Murder Is Secondary
(A Susan Wiles Schoolhouse Mystery)

by

Diane Weiner

For information, email **Cozy Cat Press**, cozycatpress@aol.com or visit our website at: www.cozycatpress.com

COZY CAT
PRESS

ISBN: 978-1-939816-46-7

Printed in the United States of America

Cover design by Katherine Janda
http://tea-and-jellybeans.tumblr.com

1 2 3 4 5 6 7 8 9 10

To my best friend Karen Moffett Mathis who I wish was alive to read my books. I miss her every day.

Chapter 1

"Isn't it supposed to be fall?" asked Susan Wiles. "My t-shirt is already drenched and we've barely gone half a mile." She brushed her damp blonde bangs to the side and wiped her face with the bottom of her bright teal shirt.

"You've lived in New York long enough to know the weather can be unpredictable this time of year. Give it another week or two," said her Teddy bear of a husband. "By the end of the month, it will be cooler and in another two months you'll be cursing the ice and snow." Mike glanced at his Garmin watch. "Besides, we're making progress and the heat is probably making us burn extra calories. Didn't Dr. Oz say anything about that on his shows? Anyhow, this was your idea."

"Yes, my idea," said Susan sarcastically. "It was your doctor who said you needed to exercise to lower your blood pressure."

"And yours who said you need to lose twenty pounds." Mike looked as though he regretted his words the moment they left his mouth. Susan gave him a hard swat with her sweaty hand.

"What I meant to say was that even though you look even more beautiful than you did thirty five years ago on our wedding day, we should both do everything we can to stay healthy and grow old together."

"Well, when you put it like that," said Susan. Her face softened.

"Besides, I like my women with a little meat on them." Susan gave him an even harder swat.

"We'd better keep going. I have to get to work on time," said Mike.

"How far have we gone?" asked Susan, after they had gone a bit further. The humidity was making it hard to breathe.

Mike responded, "Far enough. Let's turn around and call it a day. Besides, it smells like it's going to rain. Hang on, that's my phone." Mike took his phone out of the pocket of his basketball shorts, which hung below his belly like a hammock.

"Hey, what's up, Tank? What? What did you say?" Mike stood still. Susan saw his face turn red.

"What? Why? That's bull." Mike began walking faster and faster. Susan noticed the veins begin to pop out of his neck. "Susan and I are out walking. Let me get back home and we'll come right over." Susan quickened her pace to keep up with her husband. He ended the call and returned the phone to his pocket. The color had drained from his face.

"What's wrong?" asked Susan. She tried to keep up with Mike. "It sounds serious."

"It was Tank and it is serious. We have to get over there right away. My buddy is in a whole lot of trouble.

Chapter 2

Susan and Mike hurried home, then jumped into Mike's black Bronco. "What kind of trouble?" asked Susan.

"I'll have to let him explain."

"What's it about?"

"I'm not sure I got it all. He was talking so fast. It sounds bad." In the small town of Westbrook, nowhere was far from anywhere else so they arrived at Tank's within minutes.

Tank Copland was pacing on the front stoop waiting for them and opened the front door before they could even make it up the steps. His hair was disheveled and it looked like he had spilled coffee on his shirt. Tank had earned his nickname during his football days. Forty years later, balding and noticeably less muscular, the nickname still stuck. They followed him into the living room.

"So, start at the beginning," said Mike. He and Susan took a seat on the floral sofa. It had been a while since she'd been here, but Susan noticed that Tank hadn't changed a thing since his wife's death.

"Well," said Tank. He took a breath as if to calm himself down. "After school, I was cleaning up the chemistry lab when I got called to the principal's office. Even at my age, you still get the heebie jeebies when you get called to the principal's office. He asks me to tell him about the Amber Bernstein situation. I'm like, "what are you talking about?" He tells me sexual harassment accusations have been made against me."

"What? You? That's bull," said Mike. "Is he out of his mind?"

"Of course, he is. I've been at Westbrook nearly twenty five years. Twenty-five years of teaching at that damn school. Now this bimbo goes and does this and I get in trouble." Tank paced around the living room as he talked.

"What the heck? Why?" asked Susan.

"Who the hell knows? She was angry that I recommended another student's project for the National Science Contest last year instead of hers. She's even madder now that the boy, Joey, actually won. You know how great that looks on college applications? Those top schools pay attention to things like that and they hardly ever choose more than one student from a school."

"No one is going to take her word over yours," said Mike.

"That's what I thought, but they say they've got something else on me. They have *evidence*."

"Evidence? What kind of evidence?" asked Susan.

"I have no fricking idea," said Tank. "I can't even fathom what it could be because there isn't any. I've done nothing wrong."

"I'll talk to Lynette right away," said Susan. Having a police detective for a daughter had opened doors in the past. She picked up her phone and tried to call Lynette but it went straight to voicemail.

"I'll help you find a good lawyer," said Mike. "They're not going to get away with this."

"You know, I volunteer over in the media center on Thursdays. I'll see what I can find out," said Susan. Mike shot her the 'don't you dare start snooping' look. She'd seen that look many times before. Both he and Lynette were always getting on her case about her sleuthing, although she knew that neither of them could deny that she was quite good at it. After all, she had been instrumental in solving her former boss's murder just a few months ago.

"Thanks," said Tank. "What would I do without you?"

Chapter 3

The next morning, Susan woke up to the aroma of freshly brewed coffee. As soon as she opened her eyes, she remembered the seriousness of Tank's situation and felt an urgency to get moving. "Move over, Johann," she said as she nudged her black cat off the bed. She decided to eat breakfast with Mike before showering, so she put on her pink slippers and headed downstairs.

"Hope you saved me some eggs," said Susan. Mike was seated at the table dressed for work and reading the paper. He had dark circles under his eyes. Susan knew he hadn't slept well. She had felt him tossing and turning all night long.

"Sure did. They're on the stove. I even threw in a few egg whites just for you."

She made herself a plate, poured some coffee into a mug that said 'Grandma in Training,' and sat down with her husband.

"So, what's our plan?" she asked. "How are we going to get Tank out of this mess?"

"I don't know. First, we're going to call Lynette at the police station and see what she thinks. It's too bad we couldn't reach her last night."

"What kind of evidence could they possibly have against Tank?" said Susan. "The man is practically a saint. Remember how he stayed at Renee's side all those months while she was sick? I don't think he's even been on a date since she died. No one will believe those accusations."

"You never know these days," said Mike. "A girl cries sexual harassment and 'Bam!' 'Throw the guy in jail.' 'Guilty until proven innocent;' that's how it is these days. Come on, you watch the news."

"I'm volunteering at the school this morning. I'm gonna nose around a little and see what I can find out."

"Oh, no you don't. Don't get mixed up in this. I know you want to help, so do I. I think we need to let the police handle this. If you want to help ask around for lawyer recommendations or bake Tank some lasagna. Wait, on second thought, nix the lasagna." Susan knew Mike hadn't married her for her cooking ability.

"Sure. I can do that." Susan hoped she sounded enthusiastic enough to appease Mike.

He gave her a kiss and locked the front door on his way out.

Susan cleared the table, filled up the cat food bowls, and ran upstairs to get ready. She was going to find out what they had on Tank one way or another. She jumped into her Prius and headed to the school. *I'm going to get to the bottom of this*, she thought, feeling a twinge of excitement in her stomach.

Chapter 4

Susan opened the heavy glass door and walked into the main building of Westbrook High where she was greeted by a friendly voice. As she took out her driver's license, she chatted with the receptionist who was behind the front counter. She'd known her for many years.

"Have I missed any good gossip since last week? I heard some buzz about a sexual harassment suit," said Susan.

"Since you asked," said the receptionist, "Rumors have been flying. The police were here yesterday. There was a hush-hush meeting behind closed doors after school. I left before it ended, but as I was getting ready to go, I heard raised voices coming from the principal's office."

"Hmm, that sounds juicy," said Susan.

"Remember, you didn't hear anything from me. Mum's the word." Mary Ellen covered her ears in a 'hear no evil' pose.

"Didn't hear a thing," said Susan. She left the office and proceeded down the hall to the media center where the media specialist was busily straightening the chairs and piling up books that had been left on the tables.

"These kids never put things back where they belong," she said. "They don't listen either. They're supposed to stay away from the construction site, but do they? No. They keep tracking dirt all over the floor."

"Don't worry, Janet. I'll get it taken care of." Knowing how obsessive-compulsive Janet was, Susan immediately got to work.

"Janet, what have you heard about the sexual harassment rumors going around the school?" said Susan.

"Oh, I hear it was that Amber girl who stirred things up. That girl's trouble. The boys swoon over her and Lord does she use that to her advantage. I've seen them copying articles for her, typing papers, doing homework. She's a real user as they used to say in my generation."

"Do the teachers like her?" asked Susan.

"No, they don't like her. I've seen her act mighty nasty to some of them. Last year, she happened to be in the media center along with Mr. Copland and the rest of her class when the principal announced over the loudspeaker that Joey Martin had won the National Science Contest. The girl went ballistic. Had herself a little temper tantrum right here in the middle of the media center. Mr. Copland––you know that man is always a gentleman. He calmly picked up my phone over on the desk and called Security. They suspended her for a few days. Hope those high-falooting colleges she's trying to get into get wind of that. Come to think of it, they won't. Amber's daddy takes care of every little problem that girl ever has."

Susan heard the turnstile at the entrance, and turned to see Julie Martin enter. Julie was an athletically-built science teacher whose dark hair stood out in contrast to her fair skin. A sprinkling of freckles across her nose and upper cheeks was partially concealed with foundation. Susan greeted her.

"Congratulations. I saw your son on *Sixty Minutes* last week. You must be so proud of him, winning that big science contest."

"Oh, I sure am. I was proud of him way before he won the contest. He makes it easy to be a single mother."

"Yes, I feel sorry for the parents of some of these kids. Some are downright disrespectful, and slobs to boot," said Susan, as she neatened a pile of books.

"Mean spirited too," added Julie. "Do you know that when Joey won the contest, one of his classmates—Amber Bernstein—wrote all over Twitter that he'd stolen her idea? Can you believe it?"

"I do believe it. Guess there's a lot of competition these days," said Susan.

"That's no excuse. That Amber girl is poison." Julie looked at her watch. "I have to get back to my classroom. Planning period goes so fast."

Chapter 5

Susan stayed in the media center, shelving books for a few more hours. Susan preferred the word *library*, like they used back when she went to school, but in reality there were as many computer resources now as there were books, so 'media center' was actually more accurate. The dust in the place was making her eyes itch. As she walked to her car, she was thinking that from what she'd heard so far today, Amber Bernstein certainly seemed capable of making false accusations against Tank. She still wondered what evidence they had other than Amber's accusation. She remembered how she had promised Mike she would talk to Lynette, so she decided to stop off at the police station. When she arrived, the first person she saw was her old sparring buddy, and her daughter's partner, Jackson Simpson.

"Well, hello there, Jessica Fletcher," said Jackson. The man had the beginnings of a paunch. He was in his thirties, but already, his dark hairline was beginning to recede.

"How's it going, Barney Fife?" said Susan.

"Everything's great. It's rather quiet here today. Lynette is in her office. Come on in." Jackson opened the counter gate and led Susan back to Lynette's office. Her daughter's small space was neat and professional. Susan eyed a spot on the desk which would eventually be perfect for her soon-to-be grandbaby's photo—maybe in a pretty silver frame.

"Hi, Mom. What brings you here? Don't you volunteer at the high school on Thursdays?" asked Lynette.

"I just came from there. I need your help. You know Dad's friend Tank? He's in a lot of serious trouble." Susan explained the situation to her daughter.

"Sexual harassment?" said Lynette. "I've known Tank my whole life. He's such a sweet man; there's no way I can imagine him doing something like that. That's awful"

"The girl who accused him has a grudge against Tank and I'm certain she's making the whole thing up. I did some investigating at the school and…"

"Investigating? Mom, we've talked about you leaving the detective work up to me." Lynette had her hands on her hips and had that stern look on her face. It didn't go well with Lynette's large pregnant belly.

"I know, but I was at the school anyway so I figured I'd gather whatever information I could."

"Mom, I'm glad you have sources." She held up her hand, anticipating Susan's protest. "Don't worry; I won't ask you to reveal them. If there isn't any evidence against Tank other than the one accusation, this will go nowhere," said Lynette.

"Well, apparently they have other evidence too, but we don't know what it is. Maybe you can do a little investigating for him."

"You told me an officer came to the school, so that means there's probably a police report. It's a slow day. I'll try to find the report and see what it says. I'll look into it while you go home and start cooking Dad a healthy dinner."

"But I may have some key insights." Susan realized that she was breaking into her pleading tone.

"Come on, Mom. You know you don't have a deputy's badge under that sweater." Susan was distracted by movement under Lynette's maternity shirt."

"The baby is moving, isn't he?" said Susan. "Can I feel?"

"Sure, Grandma. Put your hand here." Susan's heart fluttered.

Chapter 6

Home sweet home thought Susan. She plopped her keys down on the hall table and took off her jacket. Susan went upstairs and changed into yoga pants (which had never actually been worn for yoga) and an Old Navy t-shirt. Shortly after starting dinner, she heard Mike's car in the driveway and was anxious to tell him what she'd found out.

"Hi, Hon," said Mike. He gave her a peck on the cheek. Mike spent his days working at the Westbrook City Hall. "How was your day?"

"It was fine." She proceeded to tell Mike about Amber Bernstein being angry that Tank didn't pick her project for the National Science Competition. "Crazy as it sounds, revenge against Tank is probably her motive."

"Did you talk to Lynette? What other evidence do they have?" asked Mike.

"Yes, I dropped by the station. She said she was going to look into it."

After dinner, they turned on the TV.

"Mike, look. Isn't that Tank on the news? See. He's the one walking away from the camera with the sweatshirt covering his face." She turned up the volume. The news reporter was announcing that a high school teacher had been assigned to non-teaching duties while awaiting results of an investigation into alleged sexual harassment. The caption rolling at the bottom of the TV screen read, 'Veteran teacher sexually harasses female student.'

"How can they get away with that?" asked Susan. She felt the heat rise into her face. "You know they can't prove anything. Isn't that slander or something? It's only an allegation."

"According to Tank, the girl's father is a powerful attorney. I'm sure he knows just how far he can push this. I have to call Tank." Mike turned down the TV volume and called his buddy. When he finished the call, he told Susan that Tank had been reassigned to the textbook depository, away from student contact while they investigated. Susan knew the authorities must have more compelling evidence than just Amber's word, and she was determined to find out what it was.

"They won't be able to prove anything because Tank is innocent. It's just a shame he has to go through this. He's been through enough for a lifetime," said Susan.

"I know," said Mike. He shook his head as he often did when something seemed incongruous to him. "It's killing me, but I guess there's nothing we can do at this moment."

Chapter 7

"Joey, what do you want for dinner?" Julie Martin called to her teen-age son from the kitchen. Joey was in the living room texting, and at the same time following the baseball playoffs on the news.

"I don't know. Something good."

Julie loved when her son gave her such clear direction. "I'll make some spaghetti. We have leftover meatballs to go with it."

"Mom, come quick! Mr. Copland is on TV."

"Why is he on TV?" asked Julie. Joey jacked up the volume.

"What? That's crazy!" cried her son. "They're charging him with sexual harassment. They're taking him out of the classroom while they investigate."

Julie was clearly upset. Her feelings for Tank ran deeper than anyone knew.

"What the hell? There has to be some mistake," said Joey. The news was now showing Tank shielding himself with his sweatshirt. Julie's heart broke for the man on the screen. *He must be so embarrassed,* she thought.

"Aren't you going to call him and make sure he's okay?" said Joey.

"He looks a little busy right now, but I'll certainly try." The news segment had finished. Julie's heart ached for Tank, but she continued to get dinner on the table.

It was already growing dark outside. As Julie was taking plates out of the cabinet, she heard a sound coming from outside the kitchen window. She felt her stomach drop to the floor. She inched the curtains apart and peeked outside. *Wait. Was that movement she saw?* When she looked closer, she couldn't be sure. Julie had moved to

Westbrook fifteen years ago and she still jumped whenever she heard random sounds breaking the country quiet. Joey came in and took a swig of Gatorade from the bottle in the fridge.

"Is dinner almost ready? I'm starving," said Joey.

"Just a few more minutes." Julie peeked through the curtain. "Was Amber at school today?"

"Yeah. She's strutting around spouting off about what her daddy the lawyer is going to do to poor Mr. Copland. I can't stand her," said Joey.

"She was never one of my favorites either. Mr. Copland is so nice and this is so unfair." said Julie. She pictured Tank with his deep-set eyes and strong hands. She drained the spaghetti and poured it into a serving bowl. "Can you put this on the table?" she asked Joey. She herself had lost her appetite.

"Sure," said Joey. He heaped a pile of spaghetti onto his plate. Julie was amazed at how much food her son could pack away while staying in such good shape. *He certainly has his father's metabolism,* she thought. Despite scarfing down multiple helpings at every meal, Joey's father had never had a weight problem. Luckily that was about the only similarity Joey had to his father.

"Hey, did you hear all that noise going on outside today at school?" she asked Joey, changing the subject. "They started breaking ground for that new housing development they're building next to the school. I hope they'll be done with the bulldozing soon. It's insane trying to teach over that noise."

"Yeah, I heard it."

"It's going to be a long year. They're working right outside the window in my classroom." Julie cleared the table. As she was loading the dishwasher, she could have sworn she saw a light shining across the kitchen window. Again, she peered through the curtains and again she saw nothing outside. *I must be imagining things*, she thought. The parking lot was on the other side of her apartment building, so she knew she hadn't seen headlights. Still, she felt an uneasiness as she finished up in the kitchen and sat down on the couch with her laptop. *It's been a while now,* she thought. *I have to learn to stop worrying. Everything is fine now and it will stay that way.*

Chapter 8

"Have fun at the Poker game," said Susan. Mike was getting ready to go out.

"I will. It's a good thing I happened to meet that real estate developer at work the other day or we'd be postponing our weekly games for a while. Jason's colleague from the university is on a recruiting trip, so he won't be there. We would have been out a player." Jason was their daughter Lynette's husband.

"Who is this real estate developer?" asked Susan.

"His name is Zachary Chichester. He came into the office looking for blueprints to the high school. He's working on the new housing development and I guess they need to make sure the sewers and water pipes stay clear of each other, or that they don't hit something they aren't supposed to when they dig the foundations. Anyhow, he's from New Jersey and he'll be here in town for a while."

"Does he have a wife with him?"

"No, he mentioned something about a wife, but he's here by himself. He's staying at Rocking Horse Ranch."

"Well, take these kale chips with you to Jason and Lynette's. Here's some hummus dip to go with it."

"Kale chips?" said Mike. "Jason doesn't need kale chips. He's enough of a 'woose' already, being surrounded by all those nerdy college professors every day. He needs man food—maybe some chili dogs and beer. Hey, are you going to work on the blanket you started?"

"Yes, siree. It'll be crib-size before you know it." Susan gave Mike a kiss and locked the door behind him. She picked up her knitting but was soon bored. She wandered into the kitchen and remembered the can of Pringles she'd bought before they'd started their diet. She opened the canister and decided to try to help Tank out via some internet research. *I wonder what sort of evidence Amber Bernstein's father has,* she thought. She decided to start by finding some background information on Amber's family.

Well, Amber's father checks out. He actually is a successful attorney and it doesn't look like he's been personally involved in any law suits, she said to herself. She licked the salt off of her fingers and googled Amber's name next. She found nothing out of the ordinary. Amber Bernstein had organized a charity run, and her track and cross country times were on record.

She took another stack of chips out of the can and turned her attention to Tank. *Wait, what was his real first name? Something with a T.... Tony? No. Thomas? That was it.* After searching a bit, she came across a newspaper article about a Thomas Copland from years ago. The headline was "Chemistry Teacher Charged with Sexual Harassment." *That certainly is interesting. Could there be any truth to that?* she wondered. Then, quickly, she changed her mind, adding: *What's wrong with you? You know Tank better than that. Maybe she should ask Lynette to look into it.* She dumped the last of the Pringle's crumbs into her palm, finished them, rinsed off her hands, and called her daughter.

"Lynette, I wanted to see if you could look into something. I googled Tank and found a newspaper article from quite a few years ago that said he was accused of sexual harassment once before."

"That's not good, Mom, because now another girl in addition to Amber Bernstein has issued a statement against Tank. She's a current student at Westbrook. Even though he was no doubt acquitted of the accusation in the past, it casts doubt on his reputation today. That's three strikes." Of course, Lynette wouldn't divulge the new accusing girl's name.

"What's going to happen now?"

"If they can corroborate her accusation, then Tank will most likely be arrested and the case will go to trial. Don't worry too much, though. This case sounds awfully contrived to me. It's too convenient that all of a sudden there are two sets of accusations against him when for years there have been none. It will work out."

Susan wasn't so certain.

Chapter 9

Joey stormed into the house, slammed the door, and threw his backpack and gym bag on the floor. "Mom, I'm seriously going to kill Amber with my bare hands," he said.

Julie came running out of the kitchen. "What's wrong? What happened?"

"I got a call from an admissions director at MIT during lunch today. Apparently, they had received a venomous letter saying that I cheated my way to the top of my class, and that I won the National Science Contest because I had stolen the idea from another student. Thank God the admissions officer didn't buy it and called to warn me. I know it was Amber."

"That's unbelievable! I bet we can bring charges against her for this," said Julie.

"I thought about it," said Joey, "but remember her dad is a big shot lawyer and I bet he'd figure out a way to weasel out of it. Besides, I don't have the actual letter. I'll have to come up with another way to make her pay for this."

"You'd better call the other colleges you applied to and warn them that this might happen. Who knows what other trouble she's stirring up?"

"Oh, I will. She's going to get what's coming to her one way or another. I'm going to take a shower." Julie heard the familiar sound of her son punching the bathroom door. She hoped he hadn't put a hole in it again.

No one is going to interfere with my son's future, thought Julie. She rubbed her right hand over the scar on her left wrist as was her habit whenever she got upset. *I did what I did in order to give Joey a shot at a wonderful life. That girl is some piece of work. First she goes after Tank, and now my son.* Julie had grown fond of Tank Copland and hated to see him going through this. She thought about his warm smile, his clear blue eyes, and how he smelled like citrus and fresh cut grass. *Stop,* she thought. *Don't let yourself go there. You swore you'd never get involved in another relationship.*

Chapter 10

Susan walked through the doors of the media center, determined to find out who else had made accusations against Tank. Surely there would be some clues here as to who she was. As she was shelving books, one of her very favorite past students, Carolina Rogers, walked in. Susan had just recently retired from teaching elementary school music and Carolina had been an enthusiastic chorus member back in Susan's elementary school days. Carolina's mother had been the principal of Westbrook Elementary (and Susan's boss), until she was murdered during last year's holiday concert. Susan had always been fond of Carolina, but after she solved her mother's murder, she and Carolina became extremely close.

Carolina didn't resemble her mother at all. She had inherited her father's olive skin and shiny black hair. Susan gave her a big hug and exchanged pleasantries. Maybe Carolina would have some information.

"Carolina, what have you heard about this Amber Bernstein and the accusations she made against Mr. Copland?"

"Probably the same things you have. She says he told her that in order to get an 'A' in his class, she'd have to work for it—and he didn't mean by studying."

"Do you know any girls around the school who might be corroborating her story? Does Amber have any girlfriends?" asked Susan.

"Not really. She had a good friend last year—until Amber slept with her boyfriend. That was quite a drama. Amber posted embarrassing pictures of the guy—drunk and in his underwear—all over *Instagram* the very next day. Wait. She's been hanging around with that girl Peyton

Meyers a lot these days. I don't get that. Peyton follows her around like some kind of abused puppy dog."

"Peyton Myers?"

"Yes. As a matter of fact, I saw Peyton in here this morning. Look. That's her over there making copies." Peyton was a petite blond. She was dressed conservatively and wore her hair pulled back with a headband.

Susan was getting a clear and consistent picture of Amber Bernstein. She would try to have a chat with Peyton Myers to see if she could garner any more information.

"Well, Carolina, if you hear anything else, would you give me a call? Mr. Copland is my husband Mike's best friend and he's been through a lot. I'm afraid they're building a case against him and may be arresting him any day."

"I love Mr. Copland," replied Carolina. "He was so kind to me last year when my Mom died. If I hear anything I'll let you know. If anyone can help him, you can. You're the best, Mrs. W."

Susan resumed shelving books. After a while, she worked her way towards the front desk and told Janet what Lynette had said. She knew Janet was witness to a myriad of student interactions, seeing as she was in the media center day in and day out. Susan believed she had to stop Tank from being arrested and the best way to do that would be to find the other student who'd lodged an accusation of sexual harassment against him and get her to confess that she was lying.

"Well," said Janet, "Amber certainly doesn't have a lot of friends, but I wouldn't be surprised if she's holding something over someone's head in order to get them to lie and back up her story. That would be very much in character for that girl."

"Something like what?"

Janet thought about it for a few minutes then said, "Hmm, for example, something happened at the end of last year that really bothered me. Something didn't seem to fit."

"What was that?"

"There was a tight group of top students that used to come in and study everyday through their lunch time. They were always working on those advanced placement classes. Through an anonymous tip, it was discovered that some of the kids had been illegally using Adderall—you know, the drug for attention deficit disorder."

"And what was strange about that? I've heard that it's becoming a problem in many high schools and colleges. The kids take it so they can stay awake all night and study. Whatever happened to coffee and Red Bull?"

"Well," said Janet, "it's not the fact that they were using it. It's the fact that of the five kids who were taking it, four got into big-time trouble, but one girl, Peyton Myers, never did. I probably shouldn't be speculating, but after that, I began seeing Peyton with Amber—a lot. I had never seen them interacting before the incident. When they were together, it wasn't how it usually is with teenage girls. They weren't laughing, giggling, or taking selfies on their phones. They always seemed so serious together. Peyton seemed downright annoyed, maybe even scared of Amber."

"Do you think maybe Amber helped Peyton get out of trouble with the whole Adderall thing?" said Susan.

"I think it isn't all that far-fetched, but Amber wouldn't have done that out of the goodness of her heart. She would have wanted something in return."

"Are you thinking maybe Peyton issued a statement against Tank and that she was being coerced into it by Amber?"

"That's my theory. I've been media specialist here for nearly thirty years and I've learned to read these kids. If not that, then something similar."

Susan agreed that this seemed quite plausible. "Janet, isn't that Peyton over by the copy machine?"

"That's her. Smart girl, nice too. That guy next to her—that's her new boyfriend. Talk about opposites attracting—that kid was arrested for breaking and entering last year. He has his own parole officer, can you believe it? Tough guy, barely passing his classes. I don't know what Peyton sees in him."

"Maybe she thinks she can *save* him. You know how some girls think that with a little love and understanding, they can rescue these bad boys."

"Who knows? I wouldn't be surprised if he's the one who supplied the Adderall."

"This may just be the lead we're looking for," said Susan. She was determined to speak with Peyton Meyers and explore the relationship between her and Amber Bernstein.

Chapter 11

Julie locked the back door to her classroom and started for home. *Wish I didn't have to walk through all this dirt to get to my path. I'll be glad when this housing development finally gets built.* She didn't live far and it was a good way of getting in some daily exercise. Besides, this way, Joey could use the car after practice.

The sun was low in the sky and the wind was blowing colored leaves from the trees. She knew that soon the time would be changing and she'd be walking home most days in the dark. Julie felt an uneasiness today. Her skin tingled as her mind jumped to the inevitable fear that she'd been living with these past fifteen years. Was she being followed? She heard a crunch as if someone was stepping on the dry leaves behind her on the path. She turned around quickly, but no one was there. She continued, quickening her pace as she walked toward home. She heard a sound and let out an involuntary scream. She had developed quite the startle reflex. The hair on the back of her neck felt prickly. *It's just my imagination*, she thought.

Ever since Joey had appeared on *Sixty Minutes* a few weeks ago, the old terror had begun haunting her. She tried so hard not to be seen on camera but at one instant, she had turned away from one camera just to find another staring her in the face. She was only on screen for a moment—but still. As she continued, she became more certain that she was being followed. She quickened her pace even more, then went into an all-out run, nearly losing her shoe in the process. *Of course, today would be the day I forget my sneakers,* she thought. And now it was starting to rain. Great. She'd left her rain jacket and umbrella in her classroom. Just a few more minutes and she'd be home. The sun continued to sink into the mountains, but Julie made it home before it grew dark. She locked the door behind her, caught her breath, and turned on the lights. Should she call the police? And say what? That she thought she was being followed home. She certainly couldn't offer an explanation as to why someone would be stalking her. If it were a robber, or a rapist—both rare phenomena in this town—he surely could have caught up to her. No, she would just sound ridiculous. Maybe she was just imagining it after all. But what if she wasn't? *Maybe I'll give Susan a call,* she thought. Her daughter is a detective. Maybe she'll come over and have an unofficial look around for me.

Chapter 12

"Look, Susan, I know this might sound crazy, but I think someone followed me on the way home. I was wondering if Lynette could come over. I don't want to call the police about this because I don't exactly know what I would say. It could be my imagination. Maybe she could look around outside."

Susan was anxious to help. She began to call Lynette but then stopped. *She's probably exhausted after working all day,* thought Susan. She and the baby need their rest. Mike isn't home yet. Maybe I'll just go by and see if I can take a look around. After all, Julie lives practically around the corner. Susan put on her sweater and headed to Julie's apartment. She called Julie on the way to tell her she was coming alone. Joey answered the door.

"Susan, thanks for coming," said Julie, appearing behind her son. "You were right—we can handle this without bothering Lynette. Here, I have a couple of flashlights. Joey's going to help us." Julie handed a flashlight to Susan and another to Joey. "I hope it doesn't rain." She grabbed her keys and they stepped outside.

"I think we should start by retracing your path back toward the school," said Susan. "Scan the ground and alongside the road as we go." The trio slowly and carefully proceeded. Streetlights kept the sidewalk well lit, but once they veered onto the dirt path, the flashlights proved to be essential.

"Hey, shine your lights over here," said Joey. "There's something shiny."

"I see it," said Julie.

He brushed leaves away from the base of an oak tree with his bare hands while the two women shined their lights at the trunk. The wind began to pick up.

"What is that?" asked Julie.

"Where?" said Susan. Joey began wiping away the dirt and leaves. He picked up an object.

"Oh, it's just an empty soda can," replied Joey. They continued along the path. Susan kicked small piles of dead leaves that were in the path, while Julie scanned the wooded area alongside it. Susan buttoned her sweater. *Maybe fall was coming after all,* she thought.

A car with its headlights on high beam passed along the road through the wooded area. Julie jumped when she heard it speed by.

"Look over here," said Susan. She shined the flashlight on an oversized boot print. "Surely your feet aren't this big," she said to Julie.

"I didn't notice that before. It looks as if someone was going toward my house."

"It must be recent," said Susan. "Look here, coming out of that puddle. There are more wet prints. It rained this afternoon. If the prints had been there earlier, they would have gotten washed away."

"It hasn't been long since Mom came home and this path hardly gets much use," said Joey.

They continued along the path until they were at the construction site and could see the back door of Julie's classroom.

"I see boot prints in the dirt heading behind those trees. It looks as if someone wanted to stay hidden until Julie passed and they could follow," said Susan. "I'm pretty sure it wasn't your imagination after all, no siree. Do you have any idea who may be following you?"

Julie hesitated and rubbed her wrist. "No, I can't think of anyone at all."

Chapter 13

Susan poured her coffee into a travel mug and headed for Westbrook High. She liked helping Janet. It made her feel useful. As she pulled into the school parking lot, she witnessed a Honda Civic going around a vintage Chevy on the main road in front of the school. The Chevy revved its engine and tried to pass the Honda. This escalated into a full blown episode of road rage.

Then the two cars pulled into the parking lot. Not surprisingly, they were students. Susan opted to stay in her car until the incident concluded. She had her cell phone in her hand in case the situation deteriorated. Both drivers got out and confronted each other. She recognized the Chevy driver. It was Danny Trapani, Peyton's boyfriend. She could tell the two drivers were screaming just by observing their body language. Danny grabbed the other driver by the neck and started repeatedly punching him in the face. Susan immediately called the front office.

By the time the principal and security officers came out, the Honda Civic driver was unconscious on the ground. The security officer took Danny away while the principal waited with the unconscious boy for the ambulance to come.

Susan got out of the car and told the principal what she had witnessed. Apparently this was not the first incident of violence in which Danny had been involved. Susan remembered what Janet had told her about Danny having a parole officer and wondered again how a smart girl like Peyton could possibly have gotten involved with a boy like this. Did he make Peyton feel safe? Did he provide a sense of security? Protection? Maybe protection from Amber?

When she entered the school, Susan saw Danny sitting in front of the principal's office. Then she watched Joey Martin come through the office. He had a seat next to Danny and appeared to be comforting him. He gave him a pat on the shoulder and was speaking too softly for Susan to hear what he was saying. Joey was one of those 'good boys.' *Why would he be acting so friendly to this hoodlum?* Eventually, Joey left, and Susan watched as the principal opened his door. The security officer came out and brought Danny into the office. Susan knew this wouldn't be an easy day for Danny Trapani.

On the way to the media center, Susan saw Julie Martin in the hallway.

"Did you hear the ambulance out there?" said Julie. "I wonder what happened this morning."

"I saw the whole thing," said Susan. "Danny Trapani and another boy had an incident of road rage in front of the school. Danny punched the other boy until he fell unconscious."

"Not again. Poor Danny just can't keep himself out of trouble. Such a shame. He was the sweetest little boy. He and Joey played on the same Little League team for years. Back then, Danny was a good student and always a smile on his face." The students were passing to their next class and the halls were fairly crowded. Suddenly, Julie froze for a moment as if she'd seen or heard something unusual.

"What's wrong, Julie?" asked Susan.

"Did you see a grown man scoot around the corner with that crowd of kids? He doesn't belong here."

"What did he look like? Are you sure he wasn't a student?"

"I didn't see his face, but he was wearing business attire. Neither students nor teachers dress like that around this school."

"Should we call security?"

"Maybe it was just a substitute that I haven't seen before. If he's new to the school he may have dressed to make a good impression or something."

"So back to the Danny story. What happened? Why is he so different now?"

"His Mom got sick—cancer. She struggled for a long time but it finally beat her. Joey was devastated. They were very close—you know how little boys adore their moms. Anyway, his Dad just couldn't cope with her death. He got into drugs, started drinking heavily. He's in and out of rehab still." Julie looked at her watch. "Gotta go. I have a class waiting for me."

As Susan was entering the media center, Carolina was exiting.

"Hey, Mrs. W. Did you hear about the commotion this morning?"

"Hey, sweetie. Yes, I saw it with my own eyes."

"That Danny is always in trouble. The kid he beat up is Amber's new boyfriend. He and Amber have been bullying Peyton Myers something fierce. Of course, Danny is Peyton's boyfriend, and anyone who knows Danny knows he's all about loyalty. I'm pretty sure he was being taunted about Peyton. That always sets him off."

"What is Peyton like? Doesn't she stand up to Amber?"

"Peyton is very sweet. Smart too. I don't understand why she even goes near Amber."

Susan helped Janet for a while, then headed home.

Janet stepped out to use the restroom. She was startled to see a grown man in a business suit standing outside the media center.

"Sir, what are you doing here? I don't see an ID badge."

"ID badge? I'm supervising the construction project. Our copier broke so I was just coming by to see if there was one in the media center that we could use."

"I don't know how you got past the front desk," said Janet firmly. "You always have to show your license. I think I'll call the office and get someone to escort you out."

"That's not necessary. I'm going. I'll try the Office Max down the road."

Janet watched the man walk down the hall past Julie Martin's classroom and go through the exit door. Then she called the office and alerted them about the stranger on campus.

Chapter 14

The alarm went off at five am. Susan hoisted herself out of bed and pulled on her sweat pants. Ludwig and Johann were cuddled on top of the bedspread. Mike was still fast asleep.

"Come on, Mike. Time to go for our walk." Susan shook her husband's shoulder.

"This is crazy. It's five am."

"I don't like it any better than you do, but since you won't be home until late tonight, we have to get our walk in now."

Mike grumbled and slowly got out of bed. "At least you get to come home and go back to sleep. I have a long day ahead of me."

"Ah, the joys of being retired," said Susan.

They locked the door behind them and set out toward the school. "Aren't we supposed to add mileage today?" he asked.

"Yes. We can do a few laps around the track when we get to the school," said Susan. The chilly morning air made them quicken the pace. They got to the school in record time and did two laps around the track as Susan had suggested.

Then they decided to go around the science building and take the short cut home. The sun was rising over the mountains and Susan switched off the headlamp she was wearing.

"You know that thing looks ridiculous, don't you?" said Mike.

"Maybe so, but it certainly is functional." She had gotten the idea from watching some teams on *The Amazing Race*. She stopped dead in her tracks. They had turned the corner of the science building and were at the dirt construction site. "What's that on the ground next to that bulldozer over there in the middle of the construction site? Is it a person?"

"That's weird," said Mike. They hurried closer. Susan spotted it first.

"Oh my God, it's...a trampled body." A motionless heap in a yellow slicker was laying in the path of the bulldozer. The person had obviously been run over. Susan felt as if she was going to vomit. This was the second dead body she'd discovered this year and this one looked particularly gruesome.

"Don't touch her," warned Mike. Susan had no intention of touching the mangled body. The body was face down and looked to be the size and shape of a woman. Mike looked for signs of life but it was obvious that this person was dead. "I'm calling Lynette right now," he said.

Susan knew that Mike felt every bit as upset as she did, but he always kept his cool during emergencies. Then Susan had a horrid thought. She felt herself turning pale and for a moment was worried that she was going to faint. "That's the back door to Julie's classroom. I hope that isn't Julie lying there. There was a School Advisory meeting last night and she was, I mean is, the faculty representative. Maybe she decided to walk home afterwards."

Mike paused for a minute. "I don't think it's her. You told me that she was spooked the other day thinking she was being followed. I doubt she'd walk home in the dark, and in the rain," said Mike.

"They only had one car and if Joey needed it last night, she might have," said Susan. Her thoughts felt like bolts of lightning striking her head from the inside. She rubbed her temple.

After a short time, Susan heard a siren. Lynette and her partner Jackson arrived. Lynette was used to seeing crime scenes, but Susan could tell that even she was a little freaked out. The medical examiner was on the scene moments later. While Lynette and Jackson secured the crime scene with tape, the medical examiner carefully turned over the body and stated the obvious: this girl was beyond saving. The crime scene investigators arrived and began taking photos. They systematically traversed the construction site and carefully began bagging potential evidence.

"I'll call the principal and have him keep this area clear," said Lynette. "The students will be starting to arrive soon. The ambulance is on the way. I'd like to get the body out of here before school starts. We don't want the students to see this. It would be terribly upsetting. Besides, we want to preserve the crime scene. What a sick way to commit murder. The perpetrator had to have had serious hatred toward his victim."

"Do you know who the victim is? I hope it's not Julie," said Susan.

"No, it isn't. We found her purse. Her license says Amber Bernstein, age seventeen. What a shame. She was just a kid."

"Oh my God," said Susan. "Amber Bernstein? What was she doing out on the construction site? How could this have happened? No one accidentally drives a bulldozer around a construction site after dark and happens to hit someone. This was intentional. How did they even get the keys? Her poor parents." Susan was speaking at a frantic pace.

"Mom, you should go home now. We have to be careful to stay clear of the crime scene."

Lynette's partner, Jackson, came up behind them.

"Looks like the trailer over there was broken into. The door was pried open and the key to the bulldozer is missing from its spot on the peg board."

"The key is still in the ignition," said Lynette. "Jackson, can you notify her parents before this gets out on social media?"

"I'm on it," said Jackson. Teachers were starting to arrive and Julie came out of the back door of her classroom. She ran toward Susan.

"What happened?" she asked. The ambulance had arrived and the EMTs carefully put the mangled body on a stretcher and carried it away.

"Who is that?" asked Julie.

"It's Amber Bernstein. This is so horrible. She was run over by a bulldozer last night," said Susan.

"I was just with her last night at the School Advisory meeting. She's the student representative. There were a dozen parents here also. I can't believe she's dead."

"What time did the meeting break up?" asked Lynette.

"Around nine," replied Julie.

"Where was the meeting held?" asked Lynette.

"It was in the media center in the main building," answered Julie.

"Then why would Amber have gone all the way to the construction site instead of out the front door of the school. It doesn't make any sense."

"Actually, I know why. The science department is big on coffee so several years ago we purchased one of those industrial-sized coffee urns. We used to joke that we'd have to fill it up twice to make it through some days, especially if there was a long-winded faculty meeting. I store it in my classroom. We always use it at the SAC meetings. Coffee and pastries, you know, an incentive to get parents to show up."

"That still doesn't explain why Amber was at the construction site," said Lynette.

"After the meeting, Amber offered to bring it back to my classroom for me. She said she had to walk home anyway since her car was in the shop. It was starting to rain so I was happy not to have to go back to my classroom."

"So, then you went home?"

"Yes. I didn't think any more about it. Oh, no—if I hadn't had Amber go to the science building, she probably wouldn't have been out there at all. I hope I'm not responsible for her death."

"She lived in that direction anyway," said Susan. "It would have been much quicker for her to take the path rather than walk along the road from the front parking lot." Mike and Jackson approached. They had been looking at the tire treads and trying to determine if it were possible that this had been a prank gone bad. Mike had worked in construction before he started working at Westbrook City Hall and was very familiar with the eccentricities of bulldozers and other construction equipment.

"Well, do you think this may have been some kind of teenage prank?" asked Lynette. "Maybe some kids decided it would be funny to break into a construction trailer, steal keys, and take a bulldozer out for a joyride," she offered. "Nothing surprises me with these kids anymore."

"I don't think so," said Mike. "I'm sure not many kids have ever had the opportunity to drive a bulldozer. It's harder than it looks. There would have been treads going all directions—backwards, all over if it was someone who had never driven one of these. Judging by the depth of the treads, it looks like someone was speeding along like a greyhound chasing a rabbit. It looks to me like someone had a very specific target."

"I'd have to agree," said Jackson. "That bulldozer was on a mission."

"Then, are you saying this was intentional?" asked Susan. "Someone deliberately set out to kill Amber? You're certain?" Susan knew that Amber was not well liked but couldn't imagine someone hating her enough to kill her.

"It sure is looking that way. We will have to go back to the station and see what the CSI team comes up with. We will also have to interview any witnesses, though I doubt anyone would have seen this occur without contacting the police," said Lynette.

"Julie, can you give me a list of the people who were at the meeting last night?" asked Jackson.

"I can give you who I remember off the top of my head, but the SAC secretary has the official attendance. She teaches Geometry in the main building."

"Thanks, I'll go talk to her," said Jackson.

A car door slammed and two frantic parents approached. The man wasn't tall, and he looked to be in his early to mid-fifties. He had dark hair tinged with just enough gray to appear distinguished. The woman was about the same age, slender, and sported an expensive-looking haircut.

"Where's my daughter? What happened to Amber? Is this a sick joke? Someone said she had been run over here last night," said the father.

"I checked her bed. She hadn't slept in it," said her mother. She was hyperventilating as she spoke. "We were at a fundraiser and got back very late last night. I didn't even think to check on her. I assumed she'd gone to bed." She covered her face with her hands.

"Where is she? Where's my daughter?" demanded the father. He was nose to nose with Lynette. His face was the color of a ripe tomato.

"Mr. and Mrs. Bernstein? Do you have ID?" asked Lynette.

"ID? Do you think we'd be this upset if that wasn't our daughter?" said Bernstein. He pulled out his wallet and shoved his license in Lynette's face. "Robert and Rebecca Bernstein."

"I'm so very sorry. There's no easy way to say this. Amber was killed last night. I'm afraid she's been taken to the medical examiner's office. I'm so sorry. It appears she was run over sometime last night. We think she was going home after the SAC meeting," said Lynette.

"Run over—by a bulldozer? Are you kidding? Dead?" Amber's mother was wailing and tears rushed down her cheeks in torrents.

"Who did this to her? I demand to know. Was it intentional?" Mr. Bernstein face was red and his fists were clenched. Susan could see the veins popping out of his neck. Being a parent herself, she couldn't imagine digesting the fact that your child had been heinously murdered.

"We don't know yet, but we will start investigating immediately," said Lynette. "It looks like it may have been intentional. Do you have any idea who might have wanted your daughter dead?"

"Absolutely not. Amber had a strong personality. Lots of her friends were jealous of her, but no one wanted her dead" said Mrs. Bernstein. Lynette pulled a wad of tissues from her pocket and offered one to Mrs. Bernstein. "Oh no. I'm going to have to tell her boyfriend, Nick. He's going to be devastated too."

"You will find the killer and he or she will never again see the light of day," said Mr. Bernstein. "That's a promise."

"I know how devastated you must be right now. If you would go home and make a list for us of anyone you think may have had it in for Amber, that would be a great starting point," said Lynette. "We found her purse but we will need you to come by and confirm her identity later on."

"I can't deal with this," said Mrs. Bernstein. "How am I going to live without my daughter? She can't be dead." She was crying so hard that she began to wheeze.

"Come on, let's go home. I'll call this private investigator we use at the firm. I'm not depending on the police to get to the bottom of this any time soon," said Mr. Bernstein. He put his arm around his wife and stormed back to the car.

"Mom, you and Dad need to go home now. There's nothing more we can do here. Jackson and I will get to work on this immediately." A crowd of onlookers was beginning to form.

Susan shivered with a sudden realization. If Amber was dead, maybe teenage jealousy could have been a motive. Teenagers were known to snap and do crazy things. Just look at how Danny Trapani had beaten up Amber's boyfriend Nick. But there was someone out there with a much stronger motive. Someone whose reputation and livelihood were being threatened by the victim. Someone with good reason for wanting Amber dead, Susan realized. That someone was Tank. Susan knew beyond a shadow of a doubt that he would never kill anyone, but the public would probably jump to that conclusion. She was surprised Amber's father hadn't already thought of it. They'd have to find the real killer before it was too late.

Chapter 15

Mike came home from work earlier than expected. After all, it had been quite an emotional day. He and Susan followed their nightly ritual of dinner followed by watching the news on TV. Susan knew the reporters would be chasing this story like a hoard of bridezillas storming the doors at a Filene's basement sale. Susan couldn't believe it had only been twelve hours since they'd found Amber's body. She plopped down on the sofa next to Mike.

"How was work? Are you holding up okay" asked Susan.

"It was fine. A little hard to concentrate given the morning we had. I can't stop thinking about Amber's poor parents."

"I know. My heart aches for them."

"By the way, my new poker buddy Zachary stopped by the office again. He's been pricing materials for the new housing development and was picking up forms for permits. Looks like he'll be in town longer than he planned. Of course, no one will be constructing anything out there until they're done with the crime scene. His wife is here now too."

"Maybe we can get together with them for dinner one night since they don't know anyone here." Susan thought a distraction might do them both good. She caught the news out of the corner of her eye. "Hey, look at the TV. That's Westbrook High." Susan turned up the volume.

A news reporter was standing in front of the taped-off crime scene at the school. Thankfully, the body had already been removed, but many bystanders remained.

The reporter shoved the microphone systematically under the noses of several of the onlookers. The comments were as expected—poor Amber, how could this happen?, I can't believe it….Most everyone knew the victim and speculations about the murderer—although not solicited—include Joey Martin, Danny Trapani, and Tank Copland. The reporter asked one of the faculty members if she thought teenage rivalries could have been the motive.

"Well," said the teacher, "I've seen some of these teenagers work themselves into real rages, especially when their reputations are at stake. I hate to say it, but lots of kids here had bones to pick with Amber Bernstein. This is so tragic."

As they were listening to the news, Susan's phone rang. It was Lynette.

"Lynette, how can that be? When?" Susan's face felt warm and she began to pick at her cuticles. "Please try. I'll tell Dad."

"What is it?" asked Mike. "What's wrong?"

"Lynette says they're bringing Tank in for questioning. They think he murdered Amber."

"Are they frickin kidding? It sure didn't take them long to finger Tank."

"Mike, this is an outrage. What should we do? Can we go down there?" Susan felt nauseous.

Mike slammed his fist into his other hand. "I'm sure they won't let us see him. We should call Lynette back and tell her to make sure his lawyer gets down there before they start questioning him. This is totally absurd. Someone has to be setting him up."

"Poor Tank. First the sexual harassment charges and now he's a murder suspect? Hasn't the poor man been through enough already?" said Susan.

"That was fast. I hope they haven't closed their minds on this. They'd better be investigating other suspects too. I'll bet that girl's father was pushing for it."

"Of course, it must have occurred to Mr. Bernstein that Tank had a motive," said Susan. "This is all circumstantial. They can't arrest someone without evidence, can they?"

"I'm calling Lynette right now," said Mike. He grabbed his phone off of the coffee table.

Susan switched the stations to see if there were any more stories about the murder, but the local newscasts were just about finished. When Mike got off the phone, he told her that a custodian had come forward and testified that he had seen Tank near the construction site, just outside Julie's back classroom door around the time of the murder. It was an eyewitness account. That's why they brought Tank in so soon."

"Mike, we have to get to the bottom of this. The witness has to be mistaken."

"I can't imagine what Tank would have been doing at the school at night, especially since he's been working at the book depository. There has to be an explanation. It must have been someone who looked like Tank."

Just when she thought things couldn't get any worse, they did. Susan's phone rang.

"That might be Lynette again," she said. It wasn't. The voice on the other end was unfamiliar. Her face turned pale as she listened. Her posture stiffened.

"Okay, we'll be right over."

"What's wrong?" asked Mike.

"That was the nursing home. My Mom just died." Susan began to sob. "The manager said that the nurse brought her dinner around five and she seemed just fine but when she came back for the tray, Mom was slumped over the food."

"Oh, I'm so sorry," said Mike. He grabbed Susan in a bear hug. "You know, not many people live to be 101 years old. She had a long and happy life." Susan began to cry harder.

"I didn't expect her to live forever, but I was hoping she'd be around long enough to meet her first great grandchild. As far as the doctor could tell, her heart just stopped beating. She went peacefully, as if that's a consolation."

Chapter 16

The day of the funeral seemed to parallel the life of Susan's mother. It was clear, sunny, and colorful with the fall leaves in their full glory. Susan knew that she was lucky to have had her mom around as long as she did, but she couldn't deny the shiver that resonated through every bone and the tears that streamed from her eyes. There was a heaviness in her chest and in the pit of her stomach. Mike put his arms around her as he led her into the church. Every pew was filled. Susan's mom was well loved throughout her life. The priest spoke about what a blessed life Emma Elizabeth Burrows had led.

"Emma will walk with Jesus in the shadow of God's eternal love as she embraces everlasting life. We pray for her soul as she enters the kingdom of God," said the priest. "In the name of the Father, the Son, and the Holy Spirit, Amen."

"Amen," echoed the congregation of friends and relatives. Those who had been raised Catholic made the sign of the cross while others simply bowed their heads. Her son Evan put his arm around his mom. Susan was glad that he was able to fly in from St. Louis for the funeral. It was comforting to be surrounded by family. They went outside to the gravesite.

Lynette and her husband Jason walked over after having tossed roses on the coffin. Lynette gave Susan a hug. Then she addressed her brother. "Hey, Evan. I'm glad you came home." She kissed him on the cheek. "I know you have your plate full at med school."

"Family comes first," said Evan.

"I wish Grandma could have been here when the baby was born. Now she'll never know her great-grandchild," said Lynette. She patted her baby bump.

"She will know," said Susan. "I'm sure of that." Her blurry eyes scanned the scene and she noticed Tank talking to Julie. Was Tank holding Julie's hand? Susan took off her bifocals, wiped her eyes and repositioned them on her nose. *I must be seeing things,* thought Susan. Tank had been miserable since Renee's death and as far as Susan knew, he hadn't so much as looked at another woman. Julie was a lovely person. She could be a great support to Tank while he was going through this. She subdued her inner matchmaker for the moment. There were bigger issues at hand. Lynette's partner, Jackson, approached with his girlfriend Theresa.

"I'm sorry for your loss," said Jackson.

"Me too," said Theresa. "I know how hard it is to lose someone you love. My grandmother died last year. She had Alzheimer's and we expected it, but still it was hard when it actually happened. I still miss her."

"I'm going to go over and see how Tank is doing. I'll be right back," said Mike. Evan followed his Dad. Julie and Joey joined the gathering and expressed their condolences.

Lynette readjusted her stance and rubbed her lower back. "Joey, by the way, have you heard any students talking about Amber's murder? I suppose the school has called in grief counselors. Are the kids overwhelmingly upset?"

"Upset? Well, let's see…she was bullying my friend Kwan constantly. Peyton Meyers seemed terrified every time Amber came near her, like she was being threatened or something. There was Harvey Klodfelter. He's the boy whose picture Amber posted on *Instagram*—the one where Harvey's in his boxer shorts, throwing up into a toilet…should I go on?"

"I assume that's a *no* then," said Lynette.

"Maybe her new boyfriend, Nick, is upset. He's the only one I can think of."

"I hate to say it, but Amber was not well liked," said Julie. "I'm not saying I'm glad she died or anything, but she did some bad things to a lot of people. Do you know she even wrote a letter to MIT trying to discredit Joey? Interfering with my son's future stepped way over the line."

"There's no excuse for murder. We will find the killer," said Lynette.

"Yes, we will," said Susan. Lynette shot her a look.

"The police department will find the killer," clarified Lynette. Mom, Jason and I will see you back at the house."

"I hope we'll see you back there too," said Susan to Jackson and Theresa.

"We'll be there." Jackson and Theresa followed Lynette and Jason to the parking lot. The wind was picking up a bit. Joey saw someone he knew from school and went to say hello. There was a burst of light, as if someone had quickly flicked a light switch on and then off.

Julie jumped. "Susan, did you see that?" asked Julie.

"See what?"

"Behind the church. From around the corner, did you see a flash of light?"

"I did," said Susan. She strained to see the spot Julie had pointed out. Then it happened again. "Wait, I just saw it now. Maybe it's a flash from a camera?"

"No offense, but I doubt the Paparazzi are here covering your mom's funeral."

"Come on. Let's check it out," said Susan. Even in the midst of her grief, she couldn't resist a mystery. She needed a diversion. Julie rubbed her wrist and shook her head.

"It could be trouble. Maybe we should leave it alone," said Julie.

"Don't be silly. Come on." They carefully made their way through the cemetery to the church. *High heels just aren't meant to be worn outdoors*, thought Susan. They carefully peeked around the corner of the church. No one was there.

"I guess it was my imagination," said Julie.

"Or whoever was there doesn't want to be discovered," said Susan.

Chapter 17

Meanwhile, at Rocking Horse Ranch, Zachary Chichester was involved in a heated discussion with his wife.

"Dalia, I told you not to follow me here," said Zachary. "I'm here on business, this isn't a pleasure trip."

"I'm having doubts as to what sort of business you're doing here," said Dalia. "I spoke to Phillip. He's been looking for you. He's your partner and he has no idea what kind of business you could possibly be attending to here. He says your firm has no project in Westbrook. He's pretty upset that you took off like you did. Don't you think you owe it to him to be honest?"

"Stay out of my business, Dalia. I'm warning you. Get in the car and head on back to New Jersey." Zachary's voice sounded like bass drum to Dalia's ears. It was loud, constant, and highly irritating.

"No, I came all this way. I think maybe I'll do a little horseback riding, or perhaps visit the spa. This is quite a lovely little resort you picked out."

"I have somewhere to be right now. If I were you, I'd pack and be gone before I return." Zachary slammed the hotel room door.

Dalia had grown quite adept at feigning bravado around Zachary, while secretly her toes were shaking inside her shoes. She had no intention of leaving. She knew Zachary was up to no good here in this little town but she didn't yet have a clue as to what it was. *Hmmm, maybe the spa isn't such a bad idea,* she thought. She changed her shirt and ran a brush through her stylishly-cut auburn hair. She'd just had her bangs trimmed before the trip. *Bangs,* she thought. They were born out of necessity but she'd grown to like them. After grabbing her key card, she went downstairs to the Rocking Horse Spa. The sign over the entrance read 'Mares and Stags Welcome.' She inquired about getting a pedicure and was pleased to find out that there had been a cancellation. She picked out a color and had a seat in the first pedicure chair.

This is quite a nice little spa, thought Dalia. The walls were all glass and from the pedicure chair she could see people on a path riding real live horses. The air smelled like warm lavender—very relaxing. She took off her shoes and socks, stuck her feet into the bubbly warm water, and had a sip of herbal tea that the receptionist had offered her. She looked at the woman in the chair next to her and started a conversation.

"I love that color. What's it called?" said Dalia.

"It's called Sienna Secret. I love it."

"It's nice to see a color that isn't just another variation of red or coral," said Dalia. "Where are you visiting from?"

"Oh, I'm not. I live here. I'm just enjoying an end of the school week pedicure. And you? Are you visiting from out of town?" asked the woman.

"Yes. I live in New Jersey. Saddle River to be exact. So do you have a hot date tonight or are those pretty toenails just for your own happiness?"

"Well," said the woman. At that moment, both women audibly gasped as they looked out the window. A man on the path appeared to be arguing with his wife or girlfriend. The women watched as the man shoved the girl, grabbed her by the shoulders, shook her, and then slapped her hard across the face. The receptionist had apparently witnessed the incident as well and quickly called security.

"That's horrible!" said Dalia. "Men who do that sort of thing ought to be castrated and thrown in jail for life."

"I totally agree," said the woman in the other chair. "How humiliating and painful that girl's life must be." Dalia saw the woman's face turn red with anger and felt her own face flush with rage. "There's never an excuse for domestic violence."

"Well, it looks like security is out there now. Even if he's intercepted this time, there will always be another and another time. Men like that need to be stopped," said Dalia.

"I agree wholeheartedly," replied her companion. "By the way, back to our conversation, it so happens I do have a date. That's the only reason I'm spending money on a pedicure during closed-shoe season. How about you? Are you here with a husband?"

"Yes, but God knows I'm not doing this for him. She rolled her eyes like a haughty teenager. Have you ever been married?" asked Dalia.

"Once, seems like a lifetime ago. Biggest mistake of my life, except that I got a wonderful son out of the deal." Her toenails were dry enough to slip into a pair of flip flops. She got up from the chair carefully.

"The color is beautiful. Enjoy your date," said Dalia.

"Thanks. I hope you enjoy your visit. My name's Julie, by the way."

"I'm Dalia. Nice to meet you." Dalia had an intuitive feeling that she and Julie would meet again.

Chapter 18

Julie had been living with the fear that someone at the SAC meeting would have noticed that she had arrived late and may have decided to tell that to the police. She was thankful that that nosy custodian hadn't seen her. It's a shame that he saw Tank though. Anyhow, tonight she was going to put all worries aside and focus on enjoying the evening.

Julie felt like a school girl. Let's see, her last real date had probably been twenty years ago. Julie and Tank had worked next door to each other for the past decade and gradually had become good friends. Tank was married when they first met, and, besides, the last thing on Julie's mind at that time would have been a relationship. Things had changed though. She had decided to take a risk.

Julie slipped into her favorite black dress, and put her newly-painted toes into a pair of strappy sandals. She had curled her hair and wore it down, but with the sides pulled up into a pearl comb. Then she made her way out to the living room.

"Hey, Joey. How do I look?"

"Mom, you look great. I'm sure you'll get Mr. Copland's mind off of the situation, at least for tonight."

"Thanks. Today's his birthday. I had to talk him into celebrating it this year. He'd wanted to stay hauled up at home like he's been doing practically every night since the murder, but then, sadly enough, he decided that he should go out this year. He told me he was worried that all the rest of his birthdays might be spent in prison. Isn't that awful?"

"That's terrible. It must really suck to be him right now. They still have other suspects, right?"

"Yes. I know they brought in Danny Trapani for questioning. What looks bad for Tank is that at first he told the police that he'd been at home, alone, watching TV all night. After the witness came forward, of course, it looked terrible that he'd lied."

"It just doesn't make much sense to me. Why was he at the school the night of the murder? Hopefully, they will find the real killer and he'll be off the hook."

There was a knock at the door. Julie took a peek in the hallway mirror, then answered the door. "Happy Birthday, Tank."

"I'm not much in the mood for celebrating, but maybe a good meal and some wine will give my mind a little break. You look great, by the way."

"Thanks, you too," said Julie. She noticed that his face looked a little thinner and his eyes drooped with fatigue. She caught another glance of herself in the mirror. Maybe she'd be able to cheer him up. "Shall we?" Tank said goodbye to Joey and they got into Tank's car. They had chosen a restaurant outside of town. Both agreed they would be more comfortable in a place where they weren't likely to be recognized. Of course, Tank had been in the news quite a bit lately. Would anyone recognize him? Julie hoped not. They followed a road that reminded Julie of the twisty straws that Joey had loved as a preschooler. She had packed one in his lunchbox every day. His preschool teacher had thought that was so cute. His preschool teacher....Julie shuddered. She still couldn't think about Joey at his ground floor preschool without imagining a blast...smoke...rubble....

"So, has Joey gotten all his applications in?" asked Tank.

"Yes. Now we play the waiting game. He really has his heart set on MIT."

"He's brilliant," said Tank. "I can't imagine him not getting in. He has the grades and great SAT scores."

"Yes, but they're looking for so much more these days. They want leadership experiences, volunteer hours, travel...."

"Well, didn't he spend last summer out in West Virginia volunteering?" asked Tank.

"Yeah. He built houses with Habitat for Humanity. The boy hardly knows which end of a hammer to hold, growing up without a father and all. I can't believe he was actually able to build houses." Julie glanced at the rear view mirror and noticed a car following rather closely behind them. Tank had noticed it also.

"That guy needs to get off my tail and turn down his high beams," said Tank. Tank sped up a bit, but so did the car behind him. "This is dangerous, him following so closely on these curvy roads at night. I hope he isn't drunk or something." Tank hit the gas to try to create space but the car sped up and remained on his tail. The two-lane road was flanked with a thick blanket of pine trees. There wasn't much shoulder to speak of. Julie felt a knot in her stomach.

"Maybe you should call the police," said Tank. He continued to speed up, but again the car followed suit. "When I can find a bit of shoulder, I'm going to pull over. See if you can get the license number as he goes by," said Tank.

Julie dialed 911, her fingers quivering as she entered the numbers. "Tank, I'm really getting scared," she said. She reached the 911 operator. "Tank, where should I tell her we are?" Julie heard the brakes screech like nails on a chalkboard. Tank abruptly pulled his car over to the side of the road. The other car sped past, nearly hitting the driver's side door. Julie tried to memorize the license number, but could barely see it in the dark.

"Tell her we're on Creaky Hollow Road, about 10 miles outside of Westbrook."

Julie repeated Tank's directions. "Yes, it was a dark colored sedan—black or maybe dark blue. I copied down the first three digits of the license plate," she told the operator. She had put the phone on speaker.

"Wait there," said the operator. "I'm sending a patrol car now."

The patrol car arrived in no time and Julie repeated the description of the car and the digits she was able to get from the license plate.

"Did the driver appear to be driving as if he were under the influence of drugs or alcohol?" asked the officer.

"No," answered Tank. "He wasn't veering off the road at all and was staying on my tail the entire time. I'd say he was quite alert and sober."

"Was he trying to pass you maybe? Did you cut him off earlier or anything like that?" asked the officer.

"No, not at all. He appeared out of nowhere and his goal appeared to be simply to stay on my tail."

"Any enemies that may have wanted to cause you trouble?"

"Well, you know I've been in the news lately as a suspect in the Amber Bernstein case. No one has confronted me about it. Wait. Maybe it was Amber's father. He sure made some vocal threats to me. I'll bet it was him."

"That sounds quite possible. We'll check him out," said the officer. "We'll get right on it. Meanwhile, we'll see if we can get anything from the digits your girlfriend got off the plates."

Girlfriend? thought Julie. *That has a nice ring to it. What am I crazy? Here we are lucky to be alive, dealing with a dreadful threat and I'm flushing at the word girlfriend.*

"Did you notice any other cars on the road? Perhaps there was a witness."

"No, I don't think so. You didn't see anyone did you?" Tank turned to Julie.

"No. No one."

"Well, try to enjoy the rest of your evening," said the officer. "We'll be in touch."

"Thank you for coming so quickly," said Tank. After the police car left, he led Julie back into his car.

"Well, that was enough excitement for one evening," said Tank. "I'll bet anything it was Amber's father."

"Yeah," said Julie. Her voice was flat and she rubbed her wrist as she answered. "Must be."

They decided to forgo the restaurant in lieu of takeout. Julie called for food during the ride back into town. When they reached her apartment, she set the table, set out a few candles, and they enjoyed a romantic dinner in spite of the night's events. All evening, they had both avoided talking about the case. When they'd almost finished eating, Julie heard the key in the front door.

"Joey, I didn't realize you were out. You said you'd be home studying, so I assumed you were in your room," said Julie. "And what's on your jeans? It looks like dirt."

"Well, umm, I needed to pick up my notes from Kwan's house." He didn't look Julie in the eye as he put the keys back on the hall table. "What are you doing here anyway? I thought you were going over to the Lotus Tree Inn?"

"We were, but there was a change of plans." Julie relayed the whole story to Joey.

"What?" said Joey, "It had to be Amber's father. The apple didn't fall far from the tree in that family. Don't worry, Mom. I'll straighten him out. No one is going to hurt you."

"Honey, I love how much you care, but leave this to the police. Mr. Bernstein may be very upset and irrational right now, but he is an educated man and he is certainly familiar with the law. Even if he was trying to scare us tonight, I don't believe he'd cross the line and physically harm anyone."

"Mom, people do all sorts of things when they're angry. You need to be careful."

"I will, and so will Mr. Copland, right?" She looked at Tank.

"That's right. But it wasn't your mom he was after; it was me."

"Joey, no one is going to hurt anyone. The police are looking into it."

"Okay, Mom. Goodnight, and Happy Birthday, Mr. Copland."

"Thanks, Joey. I think I'll be heading home. I'm a bit worn out now too."

Julie walked Tank to the door and watched him drive away. *No one is going to touch anyone I love,* thought Julie. *Never again.*

Chapter 19

Babies and Such—this had become one of Susan's favorite hangouts ever since she found out she was having a grandchild. As soon as you walked in, there were racks of miniature clothing sorted by ages and sex. Susan went to the blue side first.

"Come on, Lynette. One little ten-minute ultrasound and we could know whether to stay here in babyboy land or explore the pink racks."

"Mom. You know that Jason and I had always said we wanted to be surprised. Just be patient," said Lynette.

"It's not like knowing will change anything. That's either a little boy or a little girl in there. If we know the sex we can bond even more before he or she is born. Besides, it would make shopping for baby things infinitely easier."

"Sorry, Mom, you're just going to have to wait a few more months. We're supposed to be looking at car seats anyway. I'd say they are unisex so we'll be just fine."

"Okay, the car seats are in the back." Susan led the way through the high chairs, beyond the cribs, and to the car seat aisle.

"You know, when you were little we didn't have all this selection. Not everyone even used a car seat." They inspected the array of choices.

"How are we supposed to choose?" said Lynette. "If you read the boxes, they all have similar features."

As they were looking at the different models, Susan heard Lynette's ring tone.

"Sorry, Mom. Let me take this. Jackson was going to call me with some information this morning."

"Yes, she did say a dark sedan. The plates don't match Mr. Bernstein's? A rental? Okay, thanks, Jackson." Lynette put the phone back into her pocket.

"Was that about Tank's case?" asked Susan.

"You know I'm not supposed to discuss work with you, Mom."

"But this is different. You're not discussing work; you're sharing information with me because I asked you to help out our family friend. You know you won't win this one."

Lynette hesitated before relaying the events of the previous night. Susan's observation about Tank and Julie being romantically involved was now confirmed. Susan immediately suspected Amber's father of being the driver.

"I'll bet it was Amber's father. Am I right? He drives a dark sedan and he's been spouting his mouth off about getting revenge on Amber's killer. I know he thinks Tank killed her."

"We thought it might have been his car, but the plates didn't check out," said Lynette. "It turns out that the car was a rental."

"Well, can't you find out who rented it?" said Susan.

"Unfortunately, whoever rented it gave a fictitious license. We're all pretty trusting in this town. The rental agent didn't inspect the identification. In fact, he didn't even notice that the person had signed the paperwork 'John Doe.' How brazen is that?"

"Well, if it wasn't Amber's father, who could it have been? Do you think it was a random person who thought Tank was guilty?" asked Susan.

"I doubt it. The only person who's threatened Tank at all is Amber's father. If someone else was after Tank, I imagine he would have sent threats first. Usually these things escalate. Trying to run someone off the road would probably not have been the first course of action."

"What now?"

"The crime lab guys are going over the car. We have to wait and see if anything turns up. Meanwhile, I'll go by Julie's and see if she has anything to add."

"She'll be at work right now."

"That's right. I can wait until school lets out."

"Can we still get lunch then?"

"Sure. I'm starving. Burger Shack? Wait, you and Dad are still on your diets."

"Well, I'm sure they have salads. Burger Shack sounds good to me." Experience should have told her that she was not going to order the salad…or *just* the salad. *One little cheeseburger couldn't hurt,* she thought. It takes 3500 calories to add a pound of fat. Surely one cheeseburger would barely make a dent in her progress. She was salivating already. No sooner had they made it into the parking lot when they were accosted by Amber's parents.

"*Babies and Such*, huh? Out on a nice little shopping spree with your mom, while my daughter's killer is roaming the streets. My wife won't ever be able to go shopping with Amber again. Not for a prom dress, not for a bridal gown, and never for baby clothes. There will be no grandchildren for us." Mr. Bernstein reeked of smoke. His voice was gruff and authoritative. Once again, Susan noticed the veins popping out of his neck.

"My entire family has been taken away from me," said Mrs. Bernstein. "First Amber and now my husband. He will never be himself again and neither will I." The words were sincere, but her voice was flat and monotonous, in contrast to her husband's. It sounded as if Mrs. Bernstein was on some heavy sedatives. Susan couldn't imagine being in her shoes.

"You will pay for this," continued Mr. Bernstein. "The School Board, the Westbrook Police Department. I'll destroy them all singlehandedly if my daughter's killer isn't found soon. Incompetence will not be tolerated."

"Mr. and Mrs. Bernstein, we are doing everything we can. We will find your daughter's killer," said Lynette. Mr.

Bernstein spit at her, then grabbed his wife's hand and stormed back to his car.

Chapter 20

"So what's on your agenda today?" asked Mike. He and Susan had just finished their daily walk, and Mike was about to get into the shower and go to work. "Do you still want to have Zach and his wife over for dinner?"

"Sure. That would be nice. I'm volunteering at the school today. I'll go out to the construction site and ask him if you'd like. Do you think he'll be out there?"

"Well, he made a point of saying how hands on he was being with this project. You could try. Otherwise, I'll see him tonight at the poker game."

"His wife is probably going stir crazy at the Rocking Horse Ranch while he's at work. After I leave the school, I have to go by Julie's. She and Joey are out of town. Joey has a big cross country meet and Julie asked me to feed her cat while she's gone."

Mike finished his shower while Susan made the bed and hung up the clothes that were draped over the treadmill. Once it started getting colder, she'd be relegated to doing her exercise indoors.

"Hey, I lost five pounds this week," said Mike. Susan heard the familiar creak of the scale and began feeling guilty about yesterday's cheeseburger...and fries...and milkshake. *Boy, that Lynette is a bad influence,* she thought. Lynette could eat like a truck driver and never gain a pound. Mike had been that way too, but now his age was catching up with him and his metabolism had slowed.

"That's great, Hon. What we're doing must be working." Susan hadn't lost a single pound since they started this regime. *Men just lose faster*, she thought.

She left the house shortly after Mike did, and drove over to the school. Janet was always happy to see her and

Susan felt both useful and appreciated. Handling the media center was overwhelming for one person. At lunch time, she walked outside behind the science building and worked her way over to the construction trailer.

"Excuse me," she said. "I'm looking for Zach Chichester. Is he here today?" Both of the men in the trailer looked confused.

"There's no Zach here," answered the taller of the two.

"Oh, maybe he's not on site today. I imagine he has lots of office work to manage."

"We don't have anyone named Zach involved in this project at all," said the shorter worker.

"Are you sure? He's middle-aged, dark hair, about six feet tall," said Susan.

"No, we know everyone who's involved in this project. We've been working together for months. There definitely isn't anyone named Zach or even anyone who fits that description on our team."

Susan walked away from the trailer feeling very confused. Why would Zach claim to be involved in this project if he wasn't? And if he wasn't working on the new housing development, why was he in town? Mike would see him tonight and he could do the inviting. She was now more anxious than before to spend some time with him and his wife. Her curiosity had been aroused. She put in a few more hours at the media center, then drove to Julie's apartment. When she opened the front door, she called for Julie's cat. Susan knew better than to expect the cat to come running to her, but she figured she'd give it a try. She went into the kitchen and poured some dry food into the food bowl. Then she remembered how Julie said there was a can of cat food in the fridge which Susan was supposed to put on top of the dry as an appetizer. She stopped at the fridge door to admire the magnetic photo collection. All of them were of Joey—Joey getting the science award, Joey running, Joey blowing out candles on a birthday cake…*wait*, she thought. This is interesting—a picture of Joey and a handful of other teenagers in front of a half-built house. They were wearing t-shirts that read 'Habitat for Humanity.' In the background was an array of construction equipment, including a bulldozer. *Now that's very interesting*, thought Susan. *Who would have known that Joey may have had the opportunity to operate a bulldozer after all?* It was a stretch, but it was possible. She took out the cat food and again, to no avail, called for Misty. She didn't feel right leaving the apartment without being sure the cat was okay.

Susan went searching for Misty. She went down the hall and found Joey's bedroom. She knew that Johann and Ludwig liked hiding under the bed when strangers came over so she figured maybe this cat felt the same way. As she cooed to the cat, she got down on the floor. *Boy*, she thought, *I'd better get in some yoga classes before I start crawling around with my grandbaby.* Getting down on the floor wasn't as easy as it used to be. She lifted up the dust ruffle and peered under the bed. The cat wasn't there, but she did find something notable—something unexpected—something that might just be a motive for murder.

Her knee creaked as she held onto the bed and stood up holding this new piece of evidence. It was a thick, stapled science report. She recognized the topic—*Utilizing a Saliva-Based Screening Test to Determine the Likelihood of Developing Type 1 Diabetes.* That was the project Joey had won the science fair with. It would make sense that he'd have a copy stashed under his bed, except there was something wrong with this picture. The name on the front cover was Amber Bernstein. Was it possible that Joey had actually stolen Amber's report and claimed it as his own? He'd never do that—or would he? Amber had insisted repeatedly that Joey had stolen her work. Maybe he had killed her to keep her quiet. After all, Susan didn't know much about Joey. And the picture on the fridge—Joey had been building houses with Habitat for Humanity. He could have learned how to drive a bulldozer while volunteering.

She'd have to bring this to Lynette's attention. But how was she going to explain being under Joey's bed? She really hadn't set out to snoop. She'd been looking for Julie's cat when she happened to find Amber's report. Lynette wasn't going to believe her, no siree. Lynette would accuse her of snooping again. Maybe she'd have to look into this on her own. She remembered that she still hadn't found the cat.

Next, she checked Julie's bedroom. The cat wasn't on the bed. The bathroom door was open so she peeked in there. She didn't find the cat, but couldn't resist opening the medicine cabinet. *Hmmm*, she thought. *Now I know everyone looks in medicine cabinets when given the opportunity.* She found a bottle of Advil, floss, and a box of brown hair color. She wondered why Julie would be coloring her hair. And why would she choose this color? Susan had always thought Julie's skin was awfully fair in contrast to her dark locks. Maybe she was starting to turn gray. *God knows*, thought Susan, *those grays can be pretty stubborn to cover.* This had been a very interesting day.

Suddenly the cat came running into the bedroom, using the bed as a trampoline en route to the top of the dresser. Susan nearly jumped out of her skin. "There you are Misty. There's fresh food and water inside. Glad to see you are just fine." Susan gave the white cat a scratch between her ears, then locked the front door and headed home.

Chapter 21

"Phillip, what are you doing here?" said Dalia. Zach had left for a poker game and Dalia was enjoying a quiet evening at the Rocking Horse Ranch when there was an unexpected knock at the door.

"First of all, I missed you," said Phillip. He embraced Dalia and gave her a long, wet kiss. "Secondly, we have things to talk about. Our plan is going to fall apart if Zach stays in Westbrook doing who knows what, while he ignores our paying clients back home in Saddle River."

"I can't figure out what he's up to," said Dalia. "He'd never even mentioned Westbrook—not even once. Do you think he has a clandestine client here? Maybe he's keeping it from you so he can pocket the fees without sharing them."

"Now Dalia, Zach and I are partners. We share *everything*. We would never keep secrets from each other." Both he and Dalia laughed from the pits of their bellies. "How's he treating you? Has he touched you since he gave you that gash on your chin last month?"

"I'm fine. He won't hurt me now. I have a secret weapon to protect me. Well, maybe not a secret anymore. Let's just say Zach won't dare lay a finger on me now." Dalia was startled when she heard the door unlocking. To her surprise, Zach stepped into the room. She flinched involuntarily.

"Phillip? What are you doing here?" said Zach. He stressed the word *you*.

"I came to get you back to New Jersey. You're abandoning your clients and I can't run the firm single-handedly. I don't understand how you could pick up and skip town without saying a word to me or your clients.

What on earth are you doing here in this town? This doesn't appear to be a thriving real estate mecca if you ask me."

"I have important business here that I can't talk about. Trust me. I'll be back as soon as I wrap things up here. I'll send out an email to my clients."

"What clients? The ones who showed up for appointments didn't understand why they were the only party at the meetings they'd arranged with you. Some of them left in a huff and cancelled their contracts. You're destroying the firm. You're being extremely selfish right now."

"I told you I have things to take care of. I'll be back when I get back."

"Maybe there won't be anything to come back for," said Phillip. He slammed the door and walked out.

"You're ruining my life as well," said Dalia. "What am I supposed to live on if you destroy the company? I haven't held a job since we got married, all at your insistence. How could you be so irresponsible?"

Zach took a step forward as if he was about to punch her, but he stopped himself.

"Good boy," said Dalia. "You're learning the art of self-restraint."

"Shut up, Dalia. This respite is only temporary. You'll get everything that's owed you—all in good time."

"How was your poker game? Making friends here already, aren't you?"

"It was good to be away from here for a while." He took off his boots, then grabbed a bottle of whiskey from the mini bar. "By the way, Mike invited us over for dinner Saturday night. His wife was concerned that you'd be bored sitting alone in the hotel room while I was hard at work."

"That's so sweet," said Dalia. She was genuinely surprised that there were caring people left in this world. It was true that she couldn't stand staring at the walls for another minute. "I'd love to go."

"I'll tell him we'll be there. Meanwhile, I'm going down to the lounge. Don't wait up."

"Don't worry, I won't," said Dalia. She tried to read her novel, then flipped through the TV stations. She needed something to keep her occupied. Then she noticed that Zach had left his phone on the desk. *Spying on that old bag of wind is usually interesting*, she thought. She looked up his recent search history and found a search for the name of his first wife—Kaitlyn Chichester. There was an obituary from fifteen years ago. What brought that up? Then there was a google search for an address here in town. She copied down the address and stuck it in her purse for future reference.

Chapter 22

Susan checked the chicken parmesan and gave the pasta a stir. Mike was setting the table for six, using the vintage china that Susan had inherited from her mother. Susan missed her Mom. Alzheimer's had been slowly pulling her away from Susan for many years but there was a finality to death that couldn't be underestimated.

"The table looks elegant," said Susan. "Mom kept these dishes safely tucked away in the china cabinet. We used them only on holidays and for special occasions."

"It sure does add some class to the table. We will have to make a point of using it more often," said Mike.

"That reminds me. I'll have to stop by the bank next week. I need to close out Mom's account."

Susan had decided to invite Lynette and Jason for dinner as well. Zach already knew Jason from their poker games, and Zach's wife was more or less Lynette's age. Susan was looking forward to a pleasant evening. Lynette and Jason arrived first.

"Hi, honey. You look beautiful," said Susan. "Hi, grandbaby," she said as she bent down and addressed Lynette's baby bump. "You look beautiful too," she told Jason. She ruffed up his sandy blond hair, knowing he wouldn't be able to relax until he looked in the mirror and combed it. She and Mike were always teasing him about being such a 'pretty boy.'

"Glad you could come," said Mike. "Mom's making her chicken parmesan. I haven't eaten real food in weeks."

"Well, you're looking good, Dad. I can tell you've lost weight," said Lynette. "What a scene we had at the station this afternoon. Amber Bernstein's father was in yet again, screaming about getting even with Tank and suing the police department. He's pushing to have the trial moved up. We still don't have any good leads. Tank remains the prime and pretty much—only—suspect."

"Let's have a seat," suggested Mike.

"Lynette, I didn't want to say anything until I had a chance to investigate further, but I think Joey Martin may not be as innocent as we thought."

"Investigate further?" said Lynette. "What were you planning on doing? Bugging his house, setting up a surveillance camera, or maybe wearing a wire and getting him to confess?"

"See, Lynette. That's why I didn't say anything right away."

"Spill it, Mom."

"Well, Julie had asked me to feed her cat while she and Joey were at the cross country finals. She knows I love cats and she trusted me to watch Misty."

"Go on. Just the facts, Mom."

"Well, first I saw a photo on Julie's fridge of Joey volunteering for Habitat for Humanity. There was a bulldozer in the background of the picture. Maybe Joey has had experience driving a bulldozer after all."

"That's interesting, but we don't know that for sure," said Lynette.

"Also, I found a report under his bed. It was on the topic he won the science fair with. The only thing is, it had Amber's name on it."

"I'll skip right over the part about you looking under Joey's bed. We have no idea why he had that report." She paused. "It could be that Amber was taunting him by putting *her* name on *his* work."

Dalia and Zachary arrived. Mike made the introductions while Susan brought out canapés and a bottle of wine.

Lynette grabbed the wine glasses.

"Can I pour you some wine?" Lynette filled Zach's glass, but Dalia put her hand over the top of hers.

"No thanks. Just water for me," said Dalia. She turned to Lynette. "So when are you due?"

"The end of November. Not much longer to go."

"You know," said Susan, "we're going to have a baby shower for Lynette in a few weeks. We'd love to have you and Zach come. You know, in my day, baby showers were just for us hens, but nowadays men are included too. It's nice, don't you think? How dads take so much more of an interest in the whole pregnancy thing?"

"I beg to differ," said Mike. "Who made you grilled cheese sandwiches in the middle of the night when you had cravings? Who spent four hours at the baby store trying to pick out a comforter set?"

"Well, you were the exception." Susan gave Mike a kiss on the cheek. "That's one of the reasons I married you."

The food was ready and Susan ushered her guests into the dining room.

"Yum," said Zach. "I sure do love home cooking. Not that I get any, even when I'm at home. Dalia's idea of home cooking is popping a Lean Cuisine into the microwave."

"Well," said Susan. "I don't cook like this every night. Sometimes I'm just too busy enjoying retirement."

"At least you earned it. You did work full time for many years, didn't you? Mike said you were a teacher. Dalia here just sits home and relaxes all day long."

Susan saw Dalia shoot him the evil eye. Susan detected more anger than hurt in Dalia's expression.

She was glad that Dalia wasn't buckling under to her husband's malevolence.

"Behind every successful man is a strong woman," said Lynette. Jason nodded in agreement and squeezed Lynette's hand.

"So how do you spend your days?" asked Lynette.

"I'm a real estate developer. I'm in town overseeing the construction of the new housing development that's going up behind the high school," replied Zach.

"So, you're out there behind the school most days? Hands on supervision?" said Susan.

She couldn't wait to hear his response.

"That's right. Out there in the trenches, making sure things are being done right."

Susan knew he was lying. The guys at the construction site had never even heard of Zach. She wondered what his game was.

"So, how about those Jets?" said Mike, changing the subject.

"Oh, no. Dallas Cowboys all the way," said Zach.

"Why the Cowboys? Are you originally from Texas?" asked Jason.

"Born and raised," said Zach. "My Dad was a cattle farmer. I grew up on a ranch. Been a Cowboys fan since before I could walk."

Susan and Lynette began to clear the table. They put the china in the sink and Susan took the apple pie out of the refrigerator.

"Let's not tell Mr. Chauvinist out there that I bought this at Safeway," said Susan.

"Yes," said Lynette, "after all, you're retired and sit around all day doing nothing. You had plenty of time to pick fresh apples off the tree, ground your own fresh cinnamon, and whip up some fresh cream for the topping." Susan loved Lynette's sarcastic side—when it wasn't being directed toward her.

"There's something sinister about that man," said Susan. "You know, he's lying about being at the construction site. I went out there to invite him over tonight and the guys at the site had never even heard of him."

"There's definitely something shady about him," replied Lynette. "Did you notice those expensive Italian boots? How shiny they were? He hasn't been wearing those to any construction site. And who packs multiple boots for a business trip? You know that's what those construction workers wear."

"Like minds think alike," said Susan. "We'll get to the bottom of this."

"*I'll* get to the bottom of this if there's anything other than the fact that he's a lying jerk. By the way, how's that baby blanket coming along?"

Lynette and Susan brought in the pie and coffee and sat back down at the table. "So, Lynette," said Zach, "are you going to continue working after the baby is born?"

"I'll take a little time off, but we can't afford to be a one income family. Besides, my job is part of my identity," answered Lynnette. "I just hope I can find a daycare center that meets my expectations."

"Do you have child care at the police station?" asked Zach. "It's very convenient when you can take the baby with you." Susan was surprised that he'd even known on-site daycares existed.

"Oh," she said. "Do you and Dalia have children?" She had assumed they didn't.

"Dalia and I? Heavens, no. I did have a son, but he died when he was very young," said Zach. "His mother used to take him to the preschool at her work site."

"I'm so sorry," said Susan. She felt a fleeting twinge of empathy for the man.

"Don't be. It was a long time ago. I'm over it now." He shuffled in his seat. "That pie looks delicious. See Dalia. Some women actually know how to bake pies." Zach lifted his shirt and programmed something into a small machine which was no bigger than a deck of cards. "It's my insulin pump," said Zach. "I've had type 1 diabetes practically my whole life."

"I didn't know," said Susan. "We have some sugar-free ice cream in the freezer."

"This will be just great," said Zach as he grabbed a slice of pie. "It's a fallacy that diabetics can't eat sugar. That's what the pump is for."

"You know, one of the boys at Westbrook High developed a simple test for detecting the likelihood of developing diabetes," said Susan. "He even won a big award for it."

"Zach, didn't we see that on *Sixty Minutes*?" asked Dalia.

"Yes, we did. Must be one brilliant boy to have come up with that." Zach smiled.

"Zach, maybe we should be getting back to the Ranch. It's getting late. Lynnette looks sleepy. I guess pregnancy does that to you," said Dalia. They left followed by Jason and Lynette. Susan closed the door behind them. She was pretty worn out herself and couldn't wait to crawl into bed.

Chapter 23

Susan kissed Mike goodbye and nursed a second cup of coffee while reading the newspaper. Johann was curled up at her feet. She could hear Ludwig using the scratching post in the living room. An article in the newspaper caught her eye. It said that Amber Bernstein's father was in the process of suing the school board over the sexual harassment case. He insisted that the school should have gotten rid of Tank when they found he'd been previously accused of sexual harassment, and that Tank's teaching license should have been revoked. Again, Bernstein vowed to get even with his daughter's killer.

Susan was furious. This man was out for blood—Tank's blood. She had to do something. She was planning on stopping by the school to help Janet in the media center anyway. The media center had received a large, incoming book order and all those books needed to be processed. She might just happen to run into Joey. After finding that report with Amber's name on it under his bed, Susan had some unanswered questions. As she was about to leave, her phone rang. It was Lynette.

"Hi, Lynette."

"Mom, I have something important to ask you. I know this will sound strange, but do you know whether Tank carries a handkerchief or whether he uses Kleenex?"

"Why do you want to know that? He always carries a handkerchief, like a real gentleman. He joked that he carries it in case he comes upon a damsel in distress."

"Mom, the CSI team found a handkerchief at the crime scene. They were able to get DNA from it, and we have a sample from Tank already. I'm waiting for the lab report. I was hoping the answer to my question would have been no."

"Oh God, I hope it isn't Tank's."

"Me too, but how many men carry handkerchiefs these days? I'll let you know when I get the report."

Susan felt more urgency than ever to help Tank. The police already had an eye witness who saw Tank outside on the construction site the night of the murder. If the DNA on the handkerchief matched Tank's, they might have enough to make an arrest. She arrived at the school midmorning and, as expected, Janet was overwhelmed and thrilled to have the extra help. Susan picked up a box of the new books and began sticking bar codes on them.

"So, Janet, has there been any more talk about the Amber Bernstein case?"

"The gossip has been dying down. I expect it will pick up again once an arrest is made."

"Janet, do you know anything about the other sexual harassment case that Tank was accused of? Did it happen here at Westbrook?" Susan was hoping she knew.

"Yes, it was a long time ago though. Mr. Copland's wife was still alive then. The charges were dropped pretty quickly so obviously it was a bunch of hooey."

"Did you know the girl?" asked Susan.

"They tried to keep her identity secret, but I happen to know it was a girl named Samantha Black. She was trouble—kind of reminded me of Amber in fact. She went away to college, but then she moved back. She still lives in town. As a matter of fact, I don't even think she finished college. She works at the new Walmart. Last I heard, that doesn't require a college degree."

"Samantha Black—if she went to school here, I must have been her music teacher, not that I remember her."

Susan watched as Julie Martin walked into the media center. *That's right, she has planning around this time,* thought Susan. She put down the page of bar code stickers.

"Hi, Susan. Looks like a huge pile of work in front of you," said Julie.

"Yes. I'm helping Janet process this order that just came in. Looks like most of these will go in the Social Studies' section." Susan picked up a book. "Look, this has Paris on the front." She looked at the cover whimsically. "I'd love to go there some day," said Susan.

"Me too. Pretty tough to do on a teacher's salary though. Here's one about New York. At least they have the skyline correct. So often you see the skyline still including the twin towers. That just makes me sad. It's like nothing happened, like the city wasn't changed forever." Susan noted a surprising depth of emotion in her voice.

"Has Joey heard anything from any of the colleges he applied to?"

"Well, as a matter of fact—he applied for early admission to MIT and, guess what? He's in." She was grinning from ear to ear.

"Oh, Julie! How wonderful! Congratulations."

"Thanks. We're both thrilled."

"I guess that volunteer work he did for Habitat for Humanity must have helped. That's really impressive. Of course, I know he had the grades and test scores too."

"That's a given, to even be considered; you must have those things. I think the science award really set him apart," said Julie.

Susan pried further. "The Habitat for Humanity experience must have allowed him to learn all sorts of things. I'll bet he's pretty good with power tools at this point. And don't they even learn to drive bulldozers and dump trucks? They must need to clear a place to put the foundations."

"Oh no. That would have been too much of a liability. Joey didn't even have his driver's license back then," said Julie. "Driving a bulldozer is tougher than it looks. My Dad taught me how when I was growing up so I could help clear the orchards. The consequences of being an only child." *So Julie can also drive a bulldozer. How interesting,* thought Susan. She continued to press Julie for information.

"You know, I'm so impressed by that science award. How did he even get interested in finding a screening test for diabetes? It's an odd topic for a teenage boy. Most of the teenage boys I've ever met were more interested in how to improve sports performance or how to build faster cars. Even my son Evan wasn't interested in such serious topics back in high school. And he went into medicine."

"Joey's father died from complications of diabetes shortly after Joey was born."

"That explains it. Maybe he'll be responsible for finding the cure. Who knows?" *That's the second time diabetes has come up this week,* thought Susan.

"Wouldn't that be wonderful?" Julie looked at her watch. "Oops, time to go. Nice talking to you."

Susan said goodbye, then went back to the pile of work in front of her. When it got to be lunch time, she decided to leave for the day. She still had to go by the bank to close her mother's account. If she had time, maybe she'd make a quick stop at Walmart. After all, it was on the way home. As a matter of fact, it was on the way to the bank also. She decided to pick up a few baby things for Lynette, and maybe she'd just happen to run into Samantha Black.

Walmart was less crowded than usual. On weekends, it was nearly impossible to find a parking spot, but today she pulled in right in front of the entrance. Susan grabbed a basket and mapped out a strategy. She would start in the pharmacy area, work her way through electronics, shoes, then on to clothing. She was so grateful for those big nametags the workers sported. She threw some baby powder and diaper rash cream into the basket. She passed a worker named Kelly, and another couple of employees as she worked her way around the store. Then, Bingo! When she got to the shoe department, she saw a young woman in her twenties sporting a name tag that read 'Sam.'

"Excuse me," said Susan. "Do you carry rain boots?"

"Sure. They're two aisles over," answered Sam.

"Thank you. You know how slushy it can get in the winter. Sometimes you don't need those heavy, fur-lined boots. Sometimes you just need a little something to keep your feet dry."

"I understand," said Sam. "We have a nice selection." She began putting stray shoes back into their boxes and replacing them on the shelves.

"You know," said Susan, "you look familiar. Did you happen to go to Westbrook Elementary?" She was hoping to connect with this girl.

"Yes, I did, and I recognize you. You were my music teacher, Mrs. Wiles. I loved your class. Remember how you tied yarn 'karate belts' around our recorders when we passed different songs? I made it all the way to black belt. Those were some good times. Do you still teach there?"

"As a matter of fact, I just retired last year. Now I volunteer at Westbrook High. You must have gone there too."

"I did. Had some rough patches during that time. I'm rather glad those years are behind me." She looked at the floor.

"Can you take a break? I'll buy you a cup of coffee. We can sit in the McDonald's over next to the big plastic Ronald."

"Sure. I can take my fifteen-minute break now." Sam followed Susan to the counter where they ordered McCafes and then sat at a booth.

"Yeah, Westbrook High is probably not much different than when you were there. I'm pretty sure most of the teachers are the same. Did you have my friend Mr. Copland for Chemistry when you were there?" Susan noticed tension suddenly wash over Sam's face. Sam once again looked at the ground.

"Yes, I had him my junior year."

"You've probably seen on the news that he's being accused of doing some terrible things. I know Mr. Copland very well and he's totally incapable of doing what they are accusing him of." Sam fidgeted in her seat.

"Sorry to hear that but what does that have to do with me?"

"Sam, I need your help badly. I know that you brought sexual misconduct allegations against Mr. Copland when you were a student there." Susan watched Samantha's eyes narrow. "I know that the charges didn't stick, but the same thing is happening all over again. Another girl went after him with a story similar to yours."

"Really?"

"As his friend and as someone who's trying to clear his name, I need to know if there was any truth to your accusations. I know it was a long time ago and that you are more mature of a person than you were back then. I've raised two kids myself and, believe me, I know teenagers do all sorts of crazy things. I'm not judging you and I'm not trying to get you in trouble. I just want to know the truth. If he did, in fact, do the things you accused him of, and if there is any truth to the current charges, I want to get him the help he needs. If not, he doesn't deserve what's happening to him."

Sam looked down at her shoes, then slowly her eyes met Susan's. "No, Mrs. Wiles. Mr. Copland never did any of the things I accused him of. I was a troubled, mixed up kid. In fact, he tried to help me, but I resented the fact that he thought I needed help, so I retaliated and said all those horrible things." Sam began to cry. Susan reached into her purse and handed her a tissue.

"It's okay, Sam. Like I said, teenagers do all sorts of crazy things. Thank you for being honest with me."

"I'm sure that other girl is lying too. I hope things work out for him. I need to go wash my face off and get back to work." Susan said goodbye. Mission accomplished. Now she had to confirm the identity of the other girl. Janet said she thought it might be Peyton Meyers.

Susan was starving so she pulled through a Wendy's on the way to the bank. She ordered a single patty without cheese and a small order of fries topped off with a Diet Coke. Leaving off the cheese would save a good hundred calories and she didn't supersize the fries when the teenager at the window presented that option. She'd have chosen a salad instead, but who could eat a salad while driving? While she was eating, Lynette called. The news wasn't good. The DNA on the handkerchief matched Tank's. They were about to issue an arrest warrant. She couldn't even finish her lunch. She pulled into the parking lot and called Mike.

"Susan, that's ridiculous. I've got to warn Tank. So what if the DNA matched Tank's? Did that mean he dropped the handkerchief the night of the murder? He could have dropped it days earlier."

"That's what I was thinking. Lynette says he never admitted to being at the construction site—ever. That means he lied to the police. It looks bad."

"I'll get with Tank. You finish up your business at the bank and I'll see you at home later." Susan collected herself, then went into the bank. She wanted to tie up her mother's affairs as quickly as possible.

Susan signed the customer service list and waited only a few minutes before a representative called her over. Susan explained that she needed to close out her mother's account and the young woman looked up the information on her computer.

"Okay, no problem. I see she had both a savings and a checking account. I'll print the forms for you to sign and it will be taken care of. What about the safety deposit box? Would you like to cancel it as well?"

Susan had almost forgotten about the box. Her mother had given her a key when she entered the nursing home years ago. Luckily, Susan had added it to her key ring and had it with her.

"Yes, I'd like to retrieve the contents and close out the rental," said Susan.

"Follow me, then." The woman ushered her behind the locked gate which led to the safety deposit boxes. Using Susan's key as well as the bank key, she opened the box and set Susan up in a small, sterile room.

"Thank you," said Susan.

"No problem. Just hit the buzzer when you're finished."

The tiny room smelled as if someone had given the table a swipe with a Clorox wipe. Susan started to go through the contents. There was an expired passport, her parents' marriage license, Dad's death certificate, a social security card, and adoption papers. *Adoption papers*? Susan did a double take as she read the cover of the agreement. What? She turned the pages and realized that these weren't just adoption papers, they were *her* adoption papers! How was this possible? For sixty-one years she had thought she knew who her parents were. To find out now that they weren't—when they were both gone, when she couldn't ask questions or get an explanation—was unbelievable.

She was having trouble processing this. She felt a chill wash through her body. All the clichés bombarded her. Why did her real mother give her up? Who was her birth father? Frantically, she searched through the packet for the names of her real parents. Her head was pounding. To her chagrin, she realized as she read that this had been a closed adoption. Would the adoption agency release the information after all these years? She didn't even know if the agency still existed. She wondered how difficult it would be to track them down, if they were even alive. There was always the internet. And, oh yeah—she had a daughter who was a detective. She felt shaky. First the news about Tank; now this?

Maybe her real mother had been a drug addict, or in jail when she had her. Maybe she'd suffered from a dreadful genetic disease and hadn't wanted to see her daughter live a life filled with doctor visits and pain only to eventually die an early death. Didn't most genetic diseases strike earlier than age 61? Phew, maybe she'd dodged a bullet. Maybe she wasn't even Scottish. Her thoughts reminded her of a song from the musical Annie…*Maybe far away, or maybe real nearby*…Snap out of it, Susan. Focus.

Did she even want to pursue this? What would be the point? Now her hands were sweating. In a way, she felt as though she'd be betraying her mother's memory by pursuing her birth mom. Susan knew herself well enough, however, to know that squelching her natural curiosity would be nearly impossible. She took a deep breath and tried to slow down her breathing and her racing heartbeat. Then she thought about her new almost-here grandbaby. What if there was some medical history that might be important? Susan gathered up all the papers and when she felt calm enough to drive, she hit the exit buzzer, signed another form, and went home.

Chapter 24

Vinny's Pizzeria was an institution in Westbrook. It was classic Italian, complete with red and white checkered tablecloths, a map of Italy on the placemats, and opera music playing in the background. The smell of garlic and oregano greeted you at the door.

Dalia arrived at noon and was seated at a table near the window. The place was buzzing. The dining room was practically full and there was a steady stream of customers at the take-out counter. She studied the menu and drank ice water while she waited for her lunch date.

"Dalia, sorry I'm late," said Phillip. He gave her a hug and sat down. "You look terrific. Small town living agrees with you. Doesn't it just make you want to dump that big old mansion back in New Jersey?"

"Someday soon," she answered.

"Where's Zach?"

"He's out horseback riding at the Rocking Horse Ranch. He said he had business to attend to this afternoon but not surprisingly, he was very evasive about what sort of business."

"He needs to finish and get back to his real job—the one that pays the bills—the one that is funding our future." He pulled out a cigarette.

"You can't smoke in here. Put that away. You need to work on quitting."

"I know, but it's harder to quit than you'd think."

"I can't even stand to look at Zach anymore. The sooner I leave him the better He'd better not screw up our plan."

"Here's the waitress. Should we splurge on a nice Italian wine?"

"None for me, thanks. I'll stick to water."

The waitress came and took their orders.

"So, Phillip, how long do you plan to stay here in town?"

"I'm going back tonight. Someone has to run the business. Why don't you come back with me? Why are you staying here anyway?"

"Call it a gut feeling, but I know Zach is up to something. I want to keep tabs on him."

The waitress brought the food to the table. Dalia offered Phillip a taste of her soup, and he reciprocated by tearing off a piece of his sub.

Dalia shook her head and contorted her face. "No thanks."

"What's wrong? You look like you're about to toss your cookies."

"Phillip, I might as well tell you. We need to speed up our plan. Six months from now, we have to be free and clear of Zach."

"What are you saying?"

"I'm pregnant. Zach thinks it's his, that's why he isn't abusing me these days—at least not physically." She watched Phillip's face closely for a reaction. He paused for a moment, then broke into a smile. Dalia felt relieved. She felt her whole body relax.

"That's fantastic news. We're going to be a family. I can't believe it."

"We're a few steps away from that at the moment, but yes, we are. I can't wait." She took a spoonful of soup. The waitress placed a black folder with the check on the table.

Dalia scanned the restaurant. A familiar-looking woman came in with a few friends and sat at the table next to Dalia and Phillip. *How do I know her?* Dalia wondered. *Oh, yes, the spa. I think she said her name was Julie.* Julie made eye contact with her, then came over to say hello.

"Dalia, right?"

"You remembered. Julie, isn't it? Nice to run into you again," said Dalia.

"It's a teacher workday. These are a few of my colleagues. It's such a rare treat to be able to go out for lunch. Usually we scarf down our lunches in the teacher planning area. This must be your husband."

Phillip intercepted by standing up and extending his hand. "I'm Phillip Bachman. Pleased to meet you." He shook their hands. "Dalia, I need to be going so I can get on the road tonight." He took out his wallet and paid the bill.

"If you don't have somewhere to be, you're welcome to join us," said Julie. "This is my friend Carol, and this is our media specialist, Janet."

"Well, maybe I'll have a cup of coffee before I leave. Do you mind Phillip?" She was getting a bit bored hanging out in her hotel room.

"Of course not. I'll touch base before I go."

Dalia had a seat at Julie's table. "Here, don't forget your jacket." She handed it to Phillip. "It's getting cooler out. Seems like fall has officially arrived."

"Yes, it has. I'm not sorry to say goodbye to the heat and humidity. It'll be Halloween soon, then Thanksgiving. The older you get, the faster the time seems to pass," said Julie.

"I'm flying out to Dallas on Columbus Day weekend to visit my son. Guess I'll pack some sweaters," said Janet.

"It's likely to be warmer out there. The weather is unpredictable out there this time of the year. I lived there when I first married my ex-husband. He was from Texas," said Julie.

"Ex-husband? I thought you had said your husband died when Joey was just a baby," said Janet. "Complications from diabetes, right? Isn't that why Joey got interested in that topic? You know Dalia, Julie's son just won a national science contest by inventing a screening test for diabetes."

"That's what I meant," said Julie. She rubbed her wrist.

"My husband is also from Texas. Everything's bigger in Texas—that was his motto. Until we moved to New Jersey," said Dalia.

"Dalia, it was a pleasure. Maybe we'll run into each other again. We have to be getting back to school," said Julie.

When Dalia got back to the Rocking Horse, she was happy to see that Zach was still out. Dalia ran through the events of the afternoon. She was thrilled that Phillip had reacted so enthusiastically to the news of her pregnancy. Things were going exactly as planned.

Then her thoughts turned to her conversation with Julie and her friends. Dalia felt as if Julie was hiding something. For one thing, why had she told Dalia that she had an ex-husband when she'd told her friends that her husband had died? And Julie had that nervous habit of rubbing her wrist. Dalia had remembered seeing that at the spa that day as well as at the restaurant. Julie had a nasty scar there. What had caused it? The scar looked like it had been there a while. Had Julie tried to slit her wrist at one time? And then there was the hair. Julie obviously took care of her appearance. She had seemed to know her way around a spa and her sense of fashion was on the mark. Then why did she do such a lousy job of dying her hair? The dark brown color was drab and unflattering to her fair skin. It seemed off. Dalia's thoughts were interrupted by the sound of the door opening. He's hooooome. Zach reminded her of Jack Nicholson's character in *The Shining. So much for a peaceful evening,* she mused.

Chapter 25

Susan was still reeling from both the news that Tank was about to be arrested, and the discovery that she had been adopted. She wasn't ready to talk about the latter yet––not even with Mike or Lynette. Besides, she didn't want to add another thing to Mike's plate right now. She had arranged to pick up Lynette at the station for lunch. Maybe that would get her mind off of the adoption. Mike had already noticed that she wasn't acting like herself these past few days. She seldom kept secrets from Mike. She hadn't yet decided if she was going to look for her real— she meant *birth*—parents. She already knew who her real parents were. Mike would encourage her to search for them because he knew she wouldn't be at peace until she had answers. He knew her awfully well.

Susan walked into the station.

"Hey, Jackson. Is Lynette around?" said Susan.

"Hey 'Jackson'? Since when do you use my real name, Miss Marple? What's wrong?"

"Nothing. I'm just a bit tired. I haven't been sleeping well these days."

"I'm sorry to hear that."

"You, on the other hand, look great—there's a spring to your step."

"And a song in my heart—must be I'm falling in love." Jackson laughed.

"You and Theresa make a great couple. I'm glad you two found each other. Are we going to be hearing wedding bells anytime soon?"

"Maybe so. I've been looking at rings."

"Jackson, that's wonderful. I'm really happy for both of you."

Lynette came out of her office.

"Any more news about Tank's arrest?" asked Susan.

"No, we're still waiting for the paperwork to go through. I feel so awful about this. I know Tank couldn't have committed murder. There has to be another explanation as to why his handkerchief was there."

"I still think Danny Trapani may have done this," suggested Susan.

"He doesn't have an alibi, but we have nothing linking him to the crime scene. No eyewitness, and no physical evidence. It's out of our hands," replied Lynette.

"I guess you're right."

"I'm starving, Mom. Let's go eat. I'm craving Chinese."

"Fortune Dragon here we come," said Susan.

Just then the door flew open. It was Amber Bernstein's father. Susan inhaled the stale smell of smoke as soon as he walked in.

"Mr. Bernstein, I'm going to lunch. I swear that we're still working on your daughter's case," said Lynette.

"That's not why I'm here. You know that I hired a private investigator. I wanted to share some information that he found with you."

"What information?"

"My private investigator found a Zip-lock bag buried under some dry leaves at the construction site. It was found near the trailer."

"Mr. Bernstein, our crime scene investigator…"

"I'm not accusing them of any incompetence. It wasn't easily visible."

"What was in the bag?" asked Lynette.

"At first, he thought it was some sort of orange-flavored candy, but then he realized that they were glucose tablets."

"Glucose tablets? Like diabetics use?"

"Yes. He interviewed the construction crew. None of them are diabetic and no one else should have been at that site."

"Do you have the bag?"

"It's right here." Bernstein pulled a plastic bag out of his pocket. It was carefully wrapped in a handkerchief. He handed it to Lynette. "We were careful not to get our prints on it. Maybe you could run it through the crime lab."

"Thank you, Mr. Bernstein. We certainly will. Please continue to keep us in the loop."

"Of course. I want to find my daughter's killer and if we combine resources, perhaps that can be accomplished." He turned abruptly and left.

"That's interesting," said Susan, watching the departing man.

"Mom, before we go to lunch, let me show you something. Come into my office."

Susan followed Lynette into her office and Lynette pulled a stack of photographs from her desk drawer. "We found this at the crime scene. The real thing is in the evidence room, but I always take photos if I think I may need to revisit something. Look."

"What is it? It looks like it came off of a keychain."

"It did. We found it on the floor of the bulldozer after Amber's body was discovered. Look closely."

"It looks like a blue star on a silver background."

"Exactly. Do you know what that logo is?"

"No. Come on, Lynette. Just tell me."

"It's the logo for the Dallas Cowboys. Dallas Cowboys? Diabetes?"

They both said it simultaneously. "Zachary Chichester."

"How on earth is he connected to Amber's death?" asked Susan.

"Well, he is involved with the construction project isn't he? I still doubt he would have been driving the bulldozer though. Not with those shiny Italian boots."

"Lynette, remember how I told you he has no connection to that project at all. I went out to the site to invite Zachary over for dinner the other day when I was at the school volunteering. None of the workers had ever seen or heard of him."

"I remember you saying that. We now have two pieces of evidence linking him to Amber's death. We also know he's been lying, and that he has a cruel side to him. Remember how he treated his wife? This may be good news for Tank."

"I felt bad for Dalia at dinner the other night."

"The thing we are lacking is motive. Tank has motive, so does Danny Trapani, for that matter. But what possible connection does Zach Chichester have to Amber, a 17-year-old high school student in a neighboring state? I'll run it by Mr. Bernstein."

"It's very puzzling. We'll have to keep investigating until we find the common link."

"Mom...."

"I mean *you'll* have to keep investigating."

"That's better," said Lynette, although as she turned away to hide it, Susan saw Lynette smile.

"Now," said Susan, "I'm thinking my grandbaby wants some eggrolls and sweet and sour chicken."

"Yes, Mom. I think so too."

Chapter 26

Dalia waited until Zach left the hotel room and then got busy. Julie obviously had had a gut reaction about domestic violence when she witnessed it at the spa. And she said her husband had been from Texas. *Is it possible?* thought Dalia. *Could Julie have been married to Zach? Is that why Zach came here?*

She pulled out her laptop and did some searching for Zach's first wife, Kaitlyn Chichester. She turned on the TV to break the silence. After digging through many false leads, she finally found a picture of Kaitlyn and studied it closely. By the time Dalia had married Zach, there were no pictures of Kaitlyn or their son Joey anywhere in the house. That should have clued her in right away as to what type of heartless person Zach was. In the past decade, she hadn't heard him mention their names—not even once. The picture she came across was old, but still the resemblance was there. *If you colored the hair brown, cut off a few inches, and added fifteen or so pounds, this could be Julie,* she thought. It was getting chilly in the room. Dalia turned up the heat and put on a sweatshirt.

Next, Dalia searched for a death certificate. Maybe Zach had lied and he hadn't been a widower after all. With minimal effort, Dalia found an obituary for both Kaitlyn and Joey. *I guess he was telling the truth about that*, she thought. Hallelujah for the internet. According to the certificate, Kaitlyn/Julie supposedly died when Zach said she did. Didn't that lady at lunch, the media specialist, say that Julie had a teenage son? And didn't she say something about Julie's son developing some sort of test for diabetes and winning some award because his dad had died from complications from the disease? Come to think of it, maybe Kaitlyn Chichester really wasn't dead in spite of the obituary.

Maybe Kaitlyn/Julie had run away to escape Zach. *I'll bet that's where that scar came from*, she thought. If she had run away, she would have had to appease her son's curiosity when he became old enough to ask questions about his father. Zach actually has diabetes. Maybe Julie was inspired by a little wishful thinking and told Joey that his father had died from it. That way he'd never go looking for him.

So that was Zach's game. He had found out that Kaitlyn/Julie and his son were still alive and he had gone looking for them. *God help them*, thought Dalia. She had endured years and years of abuse from Zach, right up until the day she had told him she was pregnant. She could only imagine the kind of abuse he must have inflicted on Julie. Maybe he was even hurting their son. That man was completely nuts. Dalia would have left him years ago, but he always threatened that he would hunt her down and kill her if she did. Besides, she'd had no means of supporting herself. That was all changing though. She'd soon be free of that monster. She needed to call Phillip and fill him in on this latest news. He'd know how to handle it.

Dalia grabbed a bottle of water from the mini-fridge and tore open a pack of peanut M&M's. She had to warn Julie. This was not going to end well for her if Zach wasn't stopped. She couldn't even remember Julie's last name. She went back to the fridge and traded the water for a miniature bourbon. Then she remembered the baby shower. Lynette's baby shower was Saturday night at Susan's house. Surely Julie would be there and she'd be blindsided when Zach walked in. Susan had invited them to the shower the night they went over there for dinner. She had to warn Julie before it was too late. She had an idea.

Dalia walked downstairs to the spa. The same receptionist was there who had been there the day she'd met Julie.

"Good evening," said Dalia as she approached the desk. "I was in here the other day."

"Yes, I remember. What can I do for you?"

"Do you remember how I was chatting with the woman in the pedicure chair who was seated next to me?"

"Yes, it appeared as if you were making a new friend," said the receptionist.

"Well, she had told me about a house for sale in her neighborhood and I forgot to take down the information. My husband and I are considering moving here. Could I possibly get some contact information so I can talk to her further?"

"I'd love to be able to help, but I'd lose my job if I shared that information."

"I understand." Dalia exited the spa but stayed just outside the door. She weighed her options while staying out of the receptionist's sight. After a while, she came up with a plan. The riding trail passed right in front of the spa's glass wall. She remembered the domestic violence scene that she and Julie had witnessed from the pedicure chairs. She went outside and looked around. Just as she had hoped, a horse was loosely tied to one of the hitching posts outside of the café. She carefully untied the horse and gave it a swat on the rear end with her purse. He ran off loudly, passing the spa window. To add fuel to the fire, Dalia let out a blood curdling scream. A group of people came running out of the café.

Right on cue, the receptionist came running outside to see what all the commotion was about. She ran off, trying to chase down the horse. While the receptionist was outside, Dalia slipped into the spa, went behind the reception desk, and pulled up the appointment calendar on the computer. Voila. There was Julie's contact information.

Dalia immediately went back to her room and called Julie's number. Without too much effort, she got Julie to agree to meet her for breakfast the next morning.

She arrived at Denny's bright and early. It wasn't long before she spotted Julie.

"Hi, Julie. I'm so glad you were able to meet."

"I'm glad you called. What a nice treat, to eat breakfast out before school." The waitress came and poured them both some coffee.

"Julie, listen carefully." Dalia leaned across the table and spoke in a stage whisper. "I have something very important to tell you."

"You sound so serious. Go ahead."

"I don't know how to start. I guess I'll just spit it out. I am quite sure that my husband Zachary is your ex-husband and I'm also quite sure that he came to town to hurt you."

"What? I don't know what you're talking about," said Julie. Julie's shoulders tensed and she shook her head.

"I mean you no harm. Believe me, I'm on your side. I know what Zachary is like. He started abusing me on our honeymoon. I'm pretty sure that he did the same to you and that you escaped by faking your own death. You're actually Kaitlyn Chichester, aren't you?'

"No, not me," said Julie." I'm Julie Martin. I do not know anyone named Zachary." Julie emphasized *do not*. Dalia remembered reading that when people lied, they tended not to use contractions.

"I'm trying to help you. I think it's ingenious that you managed to escape that psychopath. I'm sure that Zach somehow found out that you were still alive and he's here to harm you."

Julie sat back in her seat. She looked like she was going to faint. Dalia saw the blood rush away from her face. After what seemed like an eternity, Julie spoke: "Zachary is *here*? In Westbrook? Oh, my God."

Dalia placed her hand on Julie's and squeezed it.

"You're married to Zachary?" Julie asked breathlessly. Dalia nodded.

"Please listen to me," said Dalia, insistently. "I don't want you to be blindsided when he walks into that baby shower Saturday night. Susan Wiles had mentioned that she'd invited half the teachers in the town. I figured you'd be there. We need to stop this monster."

After a brief pause, Julie said, "Dalia, you're right. You're right about all of it. I don't know what to do now that he's found me. I've dreaded this moment for the past fifteen years. I have a son who I need to protect. I feel like I'm stuck in a dark corner with no way out. I wasn't imagining things after all. Someone has been stalking me. Now it all makes sense."

"Maybe you should go to the police."

"And say what? I'm pretty sure faking your own death and keeping a father apart from his son has some sort of legal consequence."

"Then we'll have to put our heads together and find another solution. This monster has to be stopped," said Dalia. "We'll talk again soon."

Chapter 27

"The house looks beautiful," said Mike. Pink and blue streamers created a canopy over the dining room table. In the center of the table, a large punch bowl supported a concoction of fruit juice, seltzer water, and lime sherbet. There was chili, cornbread, lasagna, salad....and Susan had baked cake pops covered with pastel colored icing. A crock pot full of Swedish meatballs rounded out the feast.

"We are taking a break from our diet tonight, right?" asked Mike.

"Well, one night won't kill us," said Susan. "Did you hang the streamers out on the back porch?"

"I still say it's going to be too chilly for guests to want to mingle there, but yes, I did. I also brought out our old Boom Box in case our guests want some background music."

"I just want this night to be perfect."

"It will be. You've done a fantastic job. Hey, I think I hear a car. Our first guests have arrived."

Lynette's partner and his girlfriend entered the front door.

"Jackson, Theresa, come on in. Let me take your coats. Help yourself to some punch and snacks," said Mike. Before he could close the door, Julie, Tank, and Joey came in.

"So glad you could be here. I know you have a lot on your mind right now, Tank," said Susan.

"The trial starts the day after tomorrow. I just want this to be over," said Tank.

Dalia came in next, followed by some of Lynette's colleagues from the station.

"Zach had some business to take care of, so I don't think he'll be able to make it," said Dalia. "I was worried that I'd be late—last minute phone call as I was leaving the Rocking Horse Ranch. "Is Julie here yet?"

"Yes. I saw her in the dining room." Susan watched Dalia go in that direction. She was a little surprised that Dalia had asked about Julie. She didn't realize that they knew each other. The doorbell rang and interrupted her thoughts. "Carolina, so glad you and your Aunt Becky could make it," said Susan.

"Dad's at a meeting, but he'll come by afterwards," said Carolina. Susan was so happy that Carolina's father had pulled his life together, and stepped up to the role of father after his wife's death last winter.

The guests of honor arrived. Applause broke out when Lynette and Jason came in the front door. The guests ate and mingled for a while. Then the games began.

Susan explained the first game. "Everyone has to guess the distance around Lynette's belly." After that, the men were blindfolded and had to diaper a toy doll. Jason easily won that one. Susan couldn't help laughing when Mike whispered in Susan's ear that he wasn't surprised that Jason had won, with those delicate hands. Mike often joked that *real* men had rough hands.

The doorbell rang and Mike ushered Zach Chichester into the living room where Susan was seated next to Julie. When Zach came in, Susan saw and even felt Julie freeze as if she were afraid of Zach. *Why on earth would Julie act as if she were afraid of Zach?* thought Susan. As far as she knew, Zachary Chichester and Julie Martin had never met before. Dalia walked over and put an arm around her husband Zach. Susan saw Dalia wink at Julie. Odd again.

"Julie, this is my husband, Zach," said Dalia. Susan couldn't help noticing the venomous tone Dalia used when pronouncing her husband's name.

There was a long silence during which time Zach stared at Julie, virtually ignoring his wife. Finally, Julie took a deep breath and said quickly, "Nice to meet you, Zach."

Susan noted a coolness in Julie's tone. Susan observed Dalia's eyes darting back and forth from Julie to Zach and wondered what that was about. There seemed to be tension between the parties. Dalia didn't even know Julie as far as Susan was aware, and Julie hadn't met Zach before, so this was puzzling. Suddenly, Zach extricated himself from Dalia's grasp and began a conversation with Mike and Jason, ignoring the women. Dalia followed Julie onto the patio. *Okay*, thought Susan. *I know I'm being snoopy, but I can't help wondering why Dalia seems so anxious to talk to Julie.* Susan quietly followed behind Dalia. She ducked behind the humungous oak tree, feeling painfully hard acorns under her canvas slip-ons as she strained to listen.

"I'm sorry you had to go through that. He said he wasn't coming. Are you okay? It must have been horrible, coming face to face with that abusive monster after all these years," said Dalia.

"It wasn't easy. I can't believe I ever married that man. Thank God you warned me he was in town. Now that he knows Joey and I are still alive, there's no telling what he has up his sleeve," said Julie. Julie jumped. "Hey, did you hear something?"

"No, what?"

"It sounded like someone coughing. Probably my imagination. My senses have been on overdrive with all this recent stress."

"I didn't hear anything. Don't worry," said Dalia. "Forewarned is forearmed and we've *got* this—just like we talked about. Just play it cool for now. And remember, it's two against one now. We have the upper hand."

Susan couldn't believe what she was hearing. This story topped any episode of *Dateline* she'd ever seen. It would be hard to keep quiet about this, but what would she say? That she was following one of the guests at her daughter's baby shower, and while hidden behind an oak tree, overheard this conversation? People would think she was crazy. Besides, she didn't want to cause Julie any harm, so, it was probably better not to say anything. Mike's voice startled her.

"Come in, everyone! I think it's time to open presents," called Mike. Susan quickly slipped back into the house ahead of Julie and Dalia. She'd have to find out Julie's real name, but not tonight. This was her daughter's baby shower and she was going to enjoy the evening.

Earlier in the day, Susan had decorated a rocking chair with streamers and balloons. Lynette was seated there now.

"This is incredible, Mom. I'll never forget this night," said Lynette. Jason took a seat beside her.

"Can someone keep a list of the presents and who gave them?" asked Susan.

"I'll do it," said Carolina. She was sitting on the sofa next to Joey.

Lynette opened an array of beautiful gifts—a bouncy chair, receiving blankets, a stroller, boxes of diapers, and a myriad of yellow and mint green onesies. Susan couldn't help thinking that the guests would have had an easier time shopping if they'd known the baby's sex. When they finished opening the gifts, Lynette and Jason thanked everyone. It was time for cake. Mike came out of the kitchen with a beautiful sheet cake that said 'Congratulations, Lynette and Jason.'

"I want a rose," said Lynette. It was a running joke at the Wiles' house. Every birthday, Susan and Lynette competed for the biggest, most sugary roses.

The sliding glass doors were open. It was warm in the house with all the guests present. Julie made her way out to the patio. This time, Zach followed her. They were alone on the patio.

"What on earth are you doing here?" asked Julie. "How did you find me?" She spoke in a strained whisper.

"It's kind of like seeing a ghost," said Zach. "To think, all these years, I thought you were dead. That son of ours turned out pretty bright, didn't he? I saw him on *Sixty Minutes*. I wouldn't have ever recognized him, but then there was a camera pan that zoomed in on his mom. Imagine my surprise."

"Just leave us alone. Go back to New Jersey with your wife. Better yet, go back to New Jersey without your wife. Cut the poor woman free. Joey and I are happy. Can't you just turn around and forget you ever saw me?"

"You know me better than that. And you've kept my son from me too. What will he say when he finds out his mother lied to him? You're going to pay for this, Kaitlyn."

"Are you threatening me?" Julie hesitated, then said, "Wait a minute. Now I get it. Now I know it must have been you who followed me home on the path that night. And another time, I saw lights outside my kitchen window. That was you too, wasn't it?"

"Yep. That would have been me. I had to be sure I had the right person. I had to be careful not to strike out against the wrong person. At least, that's what I was trying to avoid."

"Oh, my God! You killed Amber, didn't you? You thought it was me you were running over because Amber came out the back door of my classroom, wearing my yellow rain slicker. You bastard!" Julie was yelling now. "You saw me wearing that slicker the night you followed me home. You killed an innocent girl when you meant to kill me."

Tank came out to the porch carrying a plate of cake. "Anything wrong?" he said.

"Nothing at all," said Zach. "I was just having a nice chat with Julie here."

"Tank, let's go back inside. It's getting cold out here," said Julie. She took a deep breath, then she went in. Tank followed her. "By the way, have you seen Joey?"

"Not lately," he replied. "He seems to be a bit infatuated with that pretty girl, Carolina. Maybe they went for a walk."

Joey and Carolina had gone for a walk. They were now hidden from view—sitting on the other side of the tool shed, out of sight of the recent scene that had recently played out.

"Carolina, did you hear that?" Joey's face was red. "That was my Dad! My Dad who I thought was dead." He shook his head back and forth. "He's a monster. He killed Amber. My father is a murderer—a cold-blooded murderer." Joey punched the cement wall with his fist.

"Joey, are you okay? Your knuckles are bleeding. Try to calm down," said Carolina, touching his arm.

"I'll live. I'm just so mad. I can't calm down. My father is a *murderer.* That's bad enough, but to top it off, my Mom has been lying to me about him all these years. She told me he died from diabetes complications."

"Joey, I've been through all this myself. We never really know who our parents are. I'm sure you don't know the whole story. Your dad was making some pretty serious threats towards your mom on top of the fact that we now know he killed Amber. Your mom is in danger. We need to call the police." Carolina handed Joey a tissue to hold on his bleeding hand. "You should see a doctor, Joey. Your hand is starting to swell."

"I can't think about going to a doctor. My whole life has been a lie. How could Mom do this to me?"

"Joey, I'd be more worried about your Mom's safety right now than the fact that she lied to you. We really need to call the police. That man, if he is your dad, has quite a temper and he sounds like a real psycho. Plus, he's a cold-blooded killer. It sounds like your mom was just trying to protect you."

Joey sighed and calmed noticeably. "You're probably right. Maybe we should wait till morning to call the police. Lynette's a detective and she'll be dragged right into this. Let's not ruin her night."

"Okay. I suppose we can wait a few hours. I'll pick you up in the morning and we'll go straight to the police station before school. Let's go inside now."

"On second thought, Carolina, maybe I shouldn't go to the police. It sounds like my Mom must have faked her own and my deaths. Isn't that a crime? Mom seemed to think it was. I don't want her to wind up in jail."

"Yes, Joey, but I just thought of something else. Poor Mr. Copland is taking the blame for Amber's death. His trial starts Monday. We know now that he didn't kill Amber. This new information will clear him of the murder charge."

"You're right; we need to go to the police. Go ahead in. I need a few more minutes."

"Okay, but remember I'm only a text away. I'll sleep with my phone next to my pillow. I'll be there if you need me. Be careful."

"Thanks, Carolina."

Carolina came inside. The party was beginning to break up. Julie and Tank were looking for Joey. Dalia came inside through the sliding glass doors.

"Did you see Joey out there?" asked Julie.

"No, I didn't," said Dalia. She leaned over and whispered into Julie's ear. "Be super careful and we'll talk again soon."

"Thank you, Dalia, for looking out for me."

"Zach's reign of terror is about to end." Joey entered through the sliding door.

"Oh, there he is," said Julie. "Joey, what happened to your hand?"

"Nothing. It's just a scrape."

"Looks like more than a scrape. We need to wash it and put some ice on it as soon as we get home." Julie said goodbye to Dalia and headed toward the front door with Joey and Tank.

"That was a great party," said Tank. "Congrats again, Lynette and Jason."

All the guests decided to leave at the same time in a flurry of goodbyes and congratulations. Soon just Lynette and Jason were left.

"Thanks again, Mom. This was wonderful," said Lynette. She gave Susan a hug.

"My first baby shower. Who knew how much fun I'd been missing?" said Jason. He was still wearing the paper plate hat that one of the guests had fashioned using the pink and blue bows from the baby gifts.

Jason and Mike took the gifts out to the car while Lynette helped Susan clear the table. When they had finished, Lynette checked her phone.

"There's a voicemail from Amber's father. That's strange," said Lynette. She put the phone up to her ear and listened.

"Why was he calling you? You look upset," said Susan. "Is he making threats again?"

"No. Amber's father says he talked to his private investigator tonight and he has proof as to who killed Amber. He wants me to get in touch with him first thing in the morning."

Chapter 28

The next day, Susan and Mike came in from an early morning walk.

"I'm still worn out from last night," said Susan. "And my legs are sore."

"We got out a little earlier than usual this morning. Why don't we spend a few minutes in the Jacuzzi?"

"Now that's a great idea." She and Mike changed into bathing suits and grabbed towels. "The worst part is getting from the house to the water. It's cold this morning."

"But it will be worth it," said Mike. They opened the sliding glass door and ran to the Jacuzzi. Susan was anticipating a relaxing soak. She ran toward the pool, looked into the Jacuzzi, and screamed.

"Mike, Mike, look. Oh my God! Mike, someone's in there. Oh my God! Someone's in the Jacuzzi. He's not moving. I think he's dead." Susan gave another scream. The body was fully clothed and floating face down.

Mike yelled, "Oh my God, you're right. Don't touch him."

"Mike, who is that? Who is it? Good Lord, this can't be happening. That looks like the shirt Zachary was wearing last night at the shower. I think it's him. How did he wind up in here?" Susan was speaking quickly and pacing in a small circle across the cement.

"Oh my God. I think you're right. I haven't a clue as to why he's in our Jacuzzi. Everyone left around the same time."

"Yes, they did."

"Didn't he and Dalia take separate cars? Must be nice to have the money to rent separate cars. I remember saying goodbye to Dalia, but come to think of it, I don't specifically remember Zach leaving. You know what? We have to call 911 right away." Mike retrieved his cell phone from the patio table and made the call.

"Look. The Boom Box you set up last night is in there too. It's still plugged in with the extension cord. I'm not sure this was an accident. The Boom Box was over on the picnic table, remember?"

"Yes, like you just said, I'm the one who set it up. Don't go near him or the cord. It's still plugged in and may be dangerous."

"This is too much. First Amber gets killed, then your best friend gets arrested, and now this." Susan shook her head from side to side. *This couldn't be happening*, she thought. She felt sick to her stomach.

"Let's put some clothes on before the police get here," said Mike. They quickly threw on some clothes and soon heard a knock at the door. The paramedics arrived first.

"The body is out back," said Mike. He and Susan led them to the hot tub. The paramedics carefully managed to disconnect the Boom Box and pulled the body out of the water. When they turned him over, there was no doubt that it was Zachary Chichester. One of the paramedics started CPR while the other took out the portable defibrillator. Susan couldn't imagine how he could still be alive, but the paramedics gave a valiant effort while waiting for the police to arrive. Susan had called Lynette right after Mike called 911. Their daughter arrived almost immediately.

"Mom, are you okay? What happened? You found another dead body? Really?"

"Dad and I were going to take a soak in the Jacuzzi after our walk and that's when I saw him. This is awful." Pink and blue streamers were still strung across the porch from the night before. *This makes the scene even more surreal*, thought Susan.

"Did you hear anything strange at all last night? Did you or Dad come back to the porch after the party broke up?" Susan saw Lynette scan the area with her eyes. Her eyes fixated on the Boom Box.

"No, we were both exhausted. I put away the food and we both went right to bed."

"Where was the Boom Box? By the way, no one uses that term any more. I can't believe you still have one. How do you think it got into the hot tub?"

"It was plugged in over on the picnic table. There's no way it accidentally fell into the water from there," said Susan.

"Okay. Stay inside with Dad. Jackson and I will mark off the area and have a look around." Just then the medical examiner arrived and officially stated the obvious: Zachary Chichester was dead. Jackson took photos of the area and the paramedics carried the body away.

"Someone has to tell Dalia. She's going to be so upset and she's all alone here in town," said Susan. "Maybe Dad and I should go over to the ranch and tell her."

"Mom, Jackson and I will go. We need to ask her some questions anyway. Why don't you check up on her later in the day?"

"Okay. Call me after you leave."

"I will. Go wait inside while we finish up here."

Susan reluctantly gave the area one last look as she went inside with Mike. And she thought her life would be calm and relaxing after retirement? She was dead wrong.

Chapter 29

After they finished with the crime scene, Lynette and Jackson headed to the Rocking Horse Ranch to break the news to Dalia. Lynette always considered this to be one of the least pleasant parts of her job. Jackson knocked on the door and Dalia, still in her robe, answered holding a cup of coffee.

"Mrs. Chichester, may we come in?" said Jackson.

"Why so formal? Lynette and I are getting to be friends already. Please call me Dalia. By the way, beautiful shower last night. Come on in. Can I get you some coffee? I have a whole pot here from room service."

"Dalia, this isn't a social call. I'm so sorry but we have some terrible news," said Lynette.

"What news? What could be so bad?"

"It's your husband, Zachary. He was found dead in the Jacuzzi in the Wiles' yard this morning."

Dalia's eyes opened wide. "What? I'm not sure I understand what you're saying. I was with him last night. I left before him and got into bed before he came home. I figured he'd gone out early, or maybe had too much to drink and spent the night elsewhere."

"It looks like he was electrocuted. There was a Boom Box, still plugged in, next to him," said Lynette.

"How did he happen to fall into the Jacuzzi? It doesn't make sense," said Dalia. She began to sniffle but Lynette felt a lack of sincerity in Dalia's emotion. "Poor Zachary."

"It may not have been an accident. In fact, the Boom Box was quite a distance from the Jacuzzi. It would have been nearly impossible for it to just have fallen in."

"Are you saying it was intentional? Someone deliberately murdered my husband?" said Dalia. What is it with this town and murders?" She was beginning to sound agitated.

"That's what we're thinking," said Lynette.

"Can you think of anyone who may have wanted your husband dead? Anyone who may have benefitted from his death? Any personal or business enemies?" asked Jackson.

"Not really," said Dalia. Lynette picked up a hesitation in her voice. "His business partner, Phillip Bachman, was quite angry at him for abandoning his customers back home, but I'm sure he wouldn't have killed him over it."

"Was he in town last night?" asked Jackson.

"I'm not sure. He's been traveling back and forth between here and New Jersey trying to convince Zachary to come back to the office."

"We will need his contact information," said Jackson. He handed Dalia a small legal pad and a pen. She knew the number off the top of her head, which Lynette found a bit odd.

"Do you know why Zachary was here in Westbrook? I know he told us that he was involved in the housing project by the school, but we know for a fact that he wasn't," said Lynette.

"I have no idea. I have little interest—had little interest—in Zachary's business dealings." Dalia grabbed a tissue from the dresser. "What do you need me to do?" asked Dalia.

"Well, the medical examiner will be spending some time with the body. After that, you will be able to make arrangements. I assume you'll want to bring the body back to New Jersey."

"Yes. I'll have to contact his poor mother and his sister. They're going to be devastated."

"I'm so sorry for your loss," said Lynette. "Let me know if there's anything I can do for you."

"And here's our card. If you think of anything else that you think is important, anything at all, please give us a call," said Jackson.

"I will," said Dalia.

When they got back to the car, Lynette said, "There's something fishy there. I got the sense that she wasn't all that broken up over her husband's death."

"Well, everyone reacts in their own way to these situations, but I know what you mean. She didn't seem all that devastated."

"You know, in the few times I saw them interacting, it seemed that Zachary was very condescending toward her. Maybe she's relieved that he's gone."

"Maybe she even did it," said Jackson. "We don't know what skeletons those two had in their marital closet. She *was* there last night."

"Yes, she was. Also, Amber's father called me late last night. In all the excitement, I almost forgot. He said he had proof that Zachary Chichester killed Amber. That's motive right there. Of course, I don't know yet what that proof is. I need to talk to him. I still don't see the connection between Zach and Amber either."

"And we need to find out if that business partner of his was in town last night. It's possible that he had deeper issues with Zachary than Dalia was aware of. Let's get back to the station. We've got some work ahead of us," said Jackson.

Chapter 30

Susan was feeling restless. The morning had wiped her out emotionally. She felt like an overtired child— exhausted to the point where it was impossible to take a nap. She began pulling down the balloons and streamers, then unloaded the dishes from the dishwasher. On top of everything else that was happening, she still couldn't get the whole concept of being adopted out of her mind. She still didn't know how she felt about searching for her biological parents. It could be a frustrating endeavor if she were unable to locate them. They may even be dead. She'd need to discuss this whole adoption issue with Mike and Lynette as soon as things calmed down. *The porch is a mess*, she thought. I'm not going anywhere near the Jacuzzi, but maybe I'll sweep a bit. As she was sweeping, she came upon several deposits of cigarette ashes. *That's odd,* she thought. No one at the party smoked. At least no one that she was aware of. After she'd finished sweeping and straightening up, she decided that by now it was *later in the day*. It was time to check in on Dalia. She grabbed her jacket and headed to Rocking Horse Ranch.

"Dalia, I'm so sorry about Zach. I just stopped by to see how you were holding up," she said to Dalia upon entering her room.

"Well, I'm still a bit in shock. All those people at the shower, no one noticed anything odd at all. I can't fathom who would have wanted him dead. After all, he doesn't even know anyone here in Westbrook other than you and Mike."

"Could someone have followed him here from New Jersey? Maybe he had an angry client? Did he owe anyone money? Double cross someone on a business deal?"

"Not that I'm aware of," said Dalia. "I hope the police solve this quickly. I just want to get Zach buried and move on with my life." Susan sensed that Dalia viewed her husband's death more as an annoyance than as a tragedy. "I hope they don't try to pin this on me. I've watched enough *Dateline*—it's always the spouse. In this case, which one?"

"What do you mean, Dalia? You said 'which one'? Does Zach have an ex-wife?" Susan, of course, already knew he did, but wanted to see Dalia's reaction.

"No, of course not. I'm really stressed, that just rolled out of my mouth," said Dalia.

"So Dalia, will you be okay financially without Zach?" *Dateline*—guilty—spouse—that was always followed by the motive: a huge life insurance policy. Susan bet that Dalia would be getting a big payoff now. Maybe that policy was just recently purchased. *Stop, it,* thought Susan. Now you're getting carried away.

"Yes, I'm sure Zach left me well taken care of, thank goodness."

"Well, if you need anything, give me a call. I assume you'll be going back home now."

"As soon as they release the body. Thanks for checking on me."

"I was worried about you. Hang in there. I'll touch base with you soon."

After she left Dalia, Susan decided to stop off at the police station and see if Lynette had any updates. As she was going in, she passed Mr. Bernstein going out. He gave her a nod as he brushed by her. Susan thought that he looked very determined, like a bull charging a matador.

"Mom, what are you doing here?" said Lynette.

"I just stopped by to check on Dalia and I thought I'd say hello before I went home. What was Mr. Bernstein doing here? Did you find out what evidence his investigator had?"

"Yes, and it's great news for Tank. I'm not sure how he managed it, but Mr. Bernstein's private investigator located an eyewitness. It was a ten-year-old boy. He was out riding his bike at the construction site the night Amber was killed. He didn't come forward earlier because his parents didn't let him ride after dark. They were still at work when he was out riding so he figured they'd never know. This boy came across the bulldozer moving all crazy, so he whipped out his cell phone, zoomed in, and shot a video. There's positive proof that Zachary was driving the bulldozer and killed Amber. We have it on video. All the charges have been dropped against Tank."

"Oh, that's wonderful. Have you told him yet?" Susan was so relieved. At least one positive thing had come out of this.

"I just finished with Mr. Bernstein so I haven't had a chance yet. I can't wait to deliver the news though."

"What about the sexual harassment charges?"

"Well, we questioned some of Amber's acquaintances again. A girl named Peyton Meyers admitted that Amber was blackmailing her into making up false accusations against Tank. I think those charges are a non-issue now."

"And I just happened to run into the girl who had accused him years ago. She recanted her story as well."

"Mom? You happened to…never mind. I don't even want to know."

"I'm so happy. You go and deliver the news. I can't wait to tell Dad," said Susan. Tank's name was now completely cleared.

Chapter 31

The next day, Susan was thrilled that Tank was in the clear, but another thing dawned on her. Dalia would now have to cope with the unpleasant truth that her husband was a murderer. Lynette had broken the news to her last night. After her morning walk with Mike, Susan decided to go by and pay Dalia another visit. Dalia didn't seem as upset as Susan had imagined she would be.

"Dalia, how are you holding up?" said Susan.

"Learning the truth about Zachary yesterday was quite overwhelming. I'm still trying to process it. I don't know how to tell his mother and sister. They will be devastated. I don't want them to hear it on the news first. Making that phone call is at the top of today's agenda."

"You look exhausted. Have you eaten breakfast?" said Susan.

"No, I haven't had much of an appetite lately."

"Let's go downstairs and at least get a cup of coffee. You can practice that conversation with me first if you'd like?"

"Yes, that may help me sort out what words I'll use to inform Zach's mother that her son killed a seventeen-year-old girl by running her over with a bulldozer. Let me wash my face and run a brush through my hair. I'll be ready in a minute." Dalia closed the bathroom door behind her and Susan had a seat on the edge of the bed.

She wondered why Dalia didn't seem more confused about Zach's motive. After all, the big question mark in Susan's mind was *how was Zachary connected to Amber, a seventeen-year-old girl who'd lived hours away from him?* Susan knew that if she were in Dalia's position, that's the first question she would have had. Maybe Dalia knew more than she was saying. Maybe Amber was the product of an affair between Mrs. Bernstein and Zach. Maybe Zach had met Amber somewhere along the way and had started a May-December romance. *Now you are being completely ridiculous*, thought Susan.

As she waited for Dalia, Susan noticed a book on the floor by the nightstand. It was half-covered by the bottom of the bedspread. She picked it up, curious as to what kind of taste Dalia had in books. She looked at the cover and was shocked to find that it was the most recent edition of *What to Expect When You Are Expecting*. Lynette had the same book. *Poor Dalia*, thought Susan. She had to admit that she was surprised. Zach and Dalia hadn't struck her as a very stable couple. Certainly not stable enough to be raising a baby. But now she was going to have to raise a baby all alone. Dalia came out of the bathroom.

"I'm ready," said Dalia. "After you." She pulled the hotel room door closed behind her. She and Susan went downstairs and had a seat at a booth in the café. Susan talked Dalia into an egg white omelet with fresh fruit. *She needs to eat for her baby's sake*, thought Susan. After eating and discussing what Dalia was going to say to Zach's mother, Dalia excused herself to go to the ladies room. *It's the pregnancy*, thought Susan. She remembered having to use the ladies room all the time when she was pregnant with Lynette and Evan. Dalia had left her phone on the table and after a few minutes had gone by, a text appeared. It was from Phillip. *That was Zachary's business partner,* thought Susan. Never able to squelch her curiosity, Susan just had to read the text. It said, *going as planned. All will be perfect soon. Love you*. This completely caught Susan by surprise. If Dalia was having an affair with Zach's partner, maybe that was the motive for murder. Especially if there was a chance that the baby was Phillip's and not Zach's. *Time for another chat with Lynette,* thought Susan. She finished breakfast with Dalia and drove to the station.

Chapter 32

"Mom, we already spoke to Zach's business partner this morning. He was in his office in New Jersey. We called bright and early. He has an alibi. There was a Chamber of Commerce awards ceremony last night. Phillip presented one of the awards, and a hundred or so witnesses can place him there," said Lynette.

"But it makes sense. I saw a text that Phillip sent Dalia proving that they are romantically involved. Also, Dalia is pregnant. Maybe the baby belongs to Phillip and not Zach. Both Dalia and Phillip had something to gain from Zach's death. If Zach died, the two of them could be together and Dalia would inherit Zach's half of the business."

"Well, that's news to me, but it doesn't change the fact that Phillip Bachman has an alibi. We'll have to keep investigating. We've only just started working on this case. Be patient. The important thing is that Tank is in the clear."

"Yes, you're right. It had to have been someone at the shower though, don't you think? Dalia was there. She could have done it."

"Mom, Dalia had financial security with Zach and she has been with him all these years. Why come to Westbrook and kill him now? Especially if she's pregnant. I can't imagine her risking being caught and sent away to jail, leaving a baby behind. She's known during their entire relationship that Zach was married before and she has probably been living with his abuse from the time they got married. The timing doesn't make sense. This was a crime of passion and opportunity. No one planned to come to the shower hoping there would be a boom box near enough to the Jacuzzi so that they could murder Zach that night. Dalia could have smothered him with a pillow or put arsenic in his coffee any day of the week. She didn't need to kill him at the baby shower."

"I guess that makes sense." Susan had to admit that Lynette was probably right. She thought a little longer, and said, "Hey, what about Mr. Bernstein? He'd just found out that Zach killed his daughter. I can't think of a better motive—and talk about a crime of passion."

"He wasn't at the shower though. We would have seen him."

"He could have snuck into the back yard." *After all, he could have hidden behind the giant oak tree*, she thought.

"But he didn't know Zach would be at your house that night and he had no way of knowing where you live. If he wanted to kill Zach, he would have gone to the hotel where he was staying."

"That's true. Lynette, I just thought of something." Susan's eyes lit up. "I found cigarette butts out in the patio. No one at the shower smoked. I smelled smoke on Mr. Bernstein when he was in here the other day. Those butts could have been his. Can't you get DNA or something?"

"Again, Mom. Why would he have thought to come to your house to find Zach? I'll look into it but I don't think it's plausible. And contrary to what you see on those TV shows you watch, DNA takes a lot longer to process than you'd think"

"Well that leaves Julie. She could have felt threatened by Zach's sudden reappearance in her life. You know, they were once married." Susan found it hard to believe, however, that Julie could do such a thing. She neglected to tell Lynette that she overheard Julie admitting to Dalia that she had faked her own death. There was no need to get Julie into legal trouble.

"I suppose she is a possible suspect. I need some time to investigate. Go home, Mom. That baby blanket isn't going to knit itself. I'll take care of things here."

"All right. I can take a hint. I'll go now." She gave Lynette a hug and patted her grandbaby. She wished she could forget about the case, go home, and knit—but she knew herself better than that.

Chapter 33

"Hey Jackson. Let's take a ride over to the Bernstein's house. Get your jacket," said Lynette.

"Sure thing." Jackson was munching on a bag of barbecue-flavored potato chips. He poured the remaining crumbs into his mouth and tossed the bag in the trash. "I'll drive. If that baby keeps on growing, you won't be able to fit behind the wheel much longer."

"Tell me about it. I can't even fit into a booth at Vinny's anymore."

"You're so lucky. I'd love to be a dad. I'll bet Jason can't wait."

"He's pretty excited, just like I am. So Jackson, speaking of having a family, when are you going to propose to Theresa?"

"I found a ring that I know she'll love. I just have to think of how I'm going to ask her. You know, these days the proposal is a big deal. People come up with all sorts of creative stuff—flash mobs, hot air balloons—I'm just not that creative."

"Don't let that stop you. Jason took me out for a romantic dinner and proposed over a glass of wine. That was good enough for me. Trust me, she loves you and will be thrilled even if you texted a proposal to her. Hey, that's the house on the left." Lynette and Jackson parked in front of a three-story semi-mansion. Mrs. Bernstein answered the door. She looked as though she'd been crying. Her hair was not brushed and she wore no makeup.

"Hello, Mrs. Bernstein. We're sorry to disturb you at such a sensitive time, but we need to ask you a few questions," said Lynette.

"A few questions? If it will help me understand why on earth that man killed my daughter, ask away." They followed her into the living room and sat on the soft white sofa. "I can see you will be a mother soon yourself. I hope you never have to go through something like this. I feel like I was murdered right along with Amber that night. I feel dead inside." Her eyes teared.

"We are so sorry for your loss. I hate to bother you, but is Mr. Bernstein here?" asked Lynette. "We'd like to speak to both of you."

"No, he went to the office. It helps distract him from this whole situation."

"Mrs. Bernstein, where were you and your husband on Saturday evening?" asked Jackson.

"Saturday night? We were right here at home, watching television." She gazed down at the floor.

Lynette noticed a hesitation in her voice. Was she telling the truth?

"Neither of you left at all that night? You're sure? Do you remember what time you went to bed that night?" asked Jackson.

"We turned in around ten, no eleven. It was after *Saturday Night Live*."

"After? *Saturday Night Live* starts later than eleven," said Jackson.

Mrs. Bernstein continued to avoid eye contact. "Oh, I guess I must be mistaken. It was midnight. Yes, midnight." Lynette could see that she was confused by her jumbled responses but there was more than that. Her intuition told her that this woman was hiding something.

"Mrs. Bernstein, this is really important. What time did you and your husband go to bed that night?" asked Lynette. She was beginning to lose patience. "Try to remember."

"I don't know. I was so upset, I took a sleeping pill. I hardly remember that night at all." She slowly looked up at Lynette with her eyes glazed over.

"Then you can't say for sure that Mr. Bernstein was home all evening, can you?" asked Lynette.

"Yes. I mean no, I can't say for sure. But don't think for a minute he killed that man. My husband is a good man. He wouldn't do anything like that."

"We aren't saying he did. We are just trying to run a thorough investigation. We will need to talk to him. At this point, we're just exploring all possibilities," said Lynette. "We want to catch your daughter's killer. Thank you for your time. We'll be in touch."

As Lynette and Jackson headed to the car, Mr. Bernstein pulled up.

"Well, two birds with one stone," said Lynette

"Let's go for it."

Jackson and Lynette approached Mr. Bernstein. "Good afternoon, Mr. Bernstein. We were just chatting with your wife. Do you mind if we ask you a few question?" said Jackson.

"Of course not. Now that we know who killed Amber, I need to know why. It doesn't make any sense. I don't understand why that man would have wanted my daughter dead." His voice made a crescendo as he continued speaking. "I'm glad he's dead."

"We are looking for motive here, now that we know Zachary Chichester killed Amber. Thank you for finding the link to her murderer, by the way. If your private investigator hadn't found that eyewitness we'd still be at square one. I received your voicemail after the baby shower Saturday night. You must have been anxious to tell me your news. What did you do when you couldn't reach me?" asked Lynette.

"Nothing. I was disappointed but what could I do? I left that message and figured I'd talk to you in the morning. I was here all night with my wife."

"Mr. Bernstein, we just spoke to your wife. She said she'd taken a sleeping pill and couldn't remember much of anything. She can't verify that you were home all evening."

"What are you saying? Just what are you accusing me of?" His voice began taking on that gruff, authoritative quality. "Do you think I killed that man? I was planning on putting him away for life, but I didn't murder him. I'm a civilized man."

"Mr. Bernstein, we need you to be truthful with us. We have reason to believe you were at the crime scene Saturday night."

"I can't believe you're accusing me of this." He was practically yelling.

"We're trying to find out why your daughter was killed. Please cooperate with us. We're trying to help," said Lynette.

"All right." He took a breath and calmed down. "I did go to your Mom's house that night. I was so anxious to tell you the news, I couldn't wait until morning, but I certainly didn't kill anyone."

"How did you know where to find me?" asked Lynette.

"I went down to the police station. They wouldn't tell me where you were, but I overheard two of the officers complaining about how they were stuck working when most of the station was at your baby shower. Then I happened to see an invitation tacked to the bulletin board. You really should be more cautious. It wasn't difficult to find the house."

"Why didn't you talk to me then?" asked Lynette.

"I saw how happy everyone was. I realized it wasn't the time or place to confront you with my information. I wanted to let you enjoy the shower."

Lynette wasn't buying this sensitive side. "So you left and went home? You were never in my mother's back yard?"

"I didn't say that. Of course, I wanted to see who this monster was who killed my daughter. I walked around to the backyard and heard someone refer to Zachary Chichester by name. I wanted to confront him—I wanted to kill him—I wanted to make him suffer—but I didn't. I restrained myself and went back home."

Lynette got the sense that he was telling the truth, although she couldn't be entirely certain. "Thank you for being honest with us. We'll talk soon," said Lynette. As she and Jackson began to walk away, Mr. Bernstein called after them.

"Wait. I just remembered something that may be important. As I was sneaking back to my car, I could have sworn I saw someone moving quietly toward the house."

"Did you get a look at him?" asked Jackson.

"No, it was dark and I was anxious to get out of there. It could have just been a neighbor or something but I remember thinking it was odd," said Mr. Bernstein. "Another thing—I think it was a man. I heard him trying to stifle a cough."

"Well, sometimes the seemingly least important observations wind up cracking the case. We'll be in touch," said Lynette.

She and Jackson got into the cruiser and drove back to the station.

Chapter 34

"Mom, I have to talk to you," said Joey. He and Julie had just sat down to dinner.

"Sure. What's wrong?" said Julie. She could tell it was serious by the tone of his voice.

"The other night at the baby shower, I overheard your conversation with Zachary Chichester. Carolina and I were sitting behind the tool shed."

"What? You were there? What exactly did you overhear?" Julie's heart dropped to her feet. At that moment, her world changed.

"I heard everything. I heard that you were once married to him but that you changed your name and faked our deaths."

Julie felt like she was going to faint. She took a few deep breaths and said, "Joey, I.....I never wanted you to find out this way." She had played this scenario over and over again in her head since the day they fled from the city. Would Joey abandon her now that he knew the truth?

"Come on, Mom. Be honest. You never wanted me to find out at all."

"Joey, it was for your own good. Zachary abused me from the day we were first married. He hit me, kicked me, ridiculed and humiliated me. He was an evil, evil man."

"Mom, I can't believe you went through that."

"That wasn't the worst thing. One day, he was angry and slapped *you* across the face. You were just a toddler. I couldn't let him hurt you too. When I got the chance, I made us disappear. I thought we'd be safe here in Westbrook. I knew he would have come after us if he thought we were alive. He would have stopped at nothing to find us." said Julie.

"I figured it was something like that. The way he was talking to you, I knew he would hurt—make that kill—you if someone didn't stop him. After all, he'd already tried to kill you once. Look what he did because Amber was wearing your raincoat. He thought she was you and ran her over with a bulldozer. That was supposed to be you. What kind of lunatic does something like that anyway?"

"Lunatic is an understatement."

"I was going to talk to the police this morning, before I heard that he'd been murdered. I'm glad he's dead. I know you were just trying to protect me. I would do the same for you." He hugged her.

"I love you, Joey. You are everything to me. Now that Zach is dead, I feel at peace. All these years I lived with the worry that he might find out the truth and come after us. Now we never have to worry about that again."

"I love you too, Mom. I'll be going to MIT next year. I don't want you to be alone. You deserve someone who treats you right. Mr. Copland seems to make you happy."

"I don't want to think about you being away, but I have to admit that Tank and I are getting closer." Julie smiled, remembering how he'd referred to her as his girlfriend that night they were being chased by Zach. "Now that he has been cleared of the murder and the sexual harassment charges, and I'm completely free from Zachary, I'm thinking our relationship can finally blossom. He's a wonderful man. We've been friends for many years."

"I like Mr. Copland a lot. I hope things work out for the two of you."

"Thanks, Joey."

Chapter 35

Dalia had just finished her phone conversation with Julie. They both felt relieved and free now that Zachary was gone. She was thankful that she'd met Julie and that she had warned her about Zach being in town. She'd felt as if she had an ally. Julie was probably the only other person in the world who knew what it was like to live with Zach. She heard a knock.

"Phillip, you shouldn't be here," said Dalia when she opened the door and saw her lover. "We don't want anyone to become suspicious about us being involved."

"I couldn't help it. I wanted to see you." He embraced her and tried to kiss her but Dalia pulled back.

"I miss you too, but I think we need to be careful. You have an alibi for the night of the murder, but I was there at the party. Fortunately, there's no apparent motive for me wanting Zachary dead. As far as the world is concerned, I'm just a grieving widow. However, if the police find out I'm having an affair with my husband's business partner, or that his business partner is stealing from the company right under my husband's nose, that will cast a shadow of suspicion over us."

"I guess you're right," said Phillip. "I don't want anything to jeopardize our future—our family's future—together."

"And that's another thing. No one knows I'm pregnant yet. I figure I'll pull out that card—the poor pregnant widow thing—if and when I need to."

"What about Kaitlyn and Joey? Do you think they'll come forward and tell the police they are still alive? How will that affect the life insurance money? Won't they have a claim to it? And to Zach's half of the company?"

"I'm sure Zach must have put me as his sole beneficiary. I don't *think* it will be a problem. Julie wouldn't risk going to the police. After all, there's no reason to now."

"Alright." Phillip sat down on the bed. "Let's order some room service. I'll go back in the morning."

Chapter 36

Susan picked up Lynette on the way to Ihop. Lynette had been having cravings for chocolate chip pancakes and Susan, being the good mother that she was, decided to forgo her morning oatmeal with flaxseeds and instead take her daughter out for breakfast. She wanted to tell Lynette about finding the adoption papers and ask her how difficult it would be to find her birth parents, if she decided she wanted to go forward with a search. After inhaling the aroma of coffee and carbs, they sat down at a table, and opened their menus. Lynette could no longer comfortably fit in a booth.

"I've been craving pancakes all week," said Lynette.

"One of the perks of being retired is being able to go out for breakfast on a weekday morning," said Susan. She ordered banana nut pancakes, with bacon and sugar-free syrup.

"Lynette, I want to talk to you about something. The other day I went down to the bank to close out Grandma's accounts. I'd forgotten all about her safety deposit box, but when the lady at the bank reminded me, I decided to gather the contents and close that out also."

The waitress put a steaming carafe of coffee down on the table. Susan poured herself a cup as she tried to talk herself into continuing this story.

"When I looked inside, I found the usual things—a marriage license, a passport—but I also found something quite unexpected."

"What did you find?" asked Lynette.

"I found adoption papers. *My* adoption papers. Lynette, Grandma and Grandpa weren't my real parents. They adopted me."

"What?" said Lynette. Susan watched as Lynette's jaw literally dropped. "Did I hear what I thought I heard?"

"I couldn't believe it either. It's taken me a few days to absorb the whole thing and even be able to talk about it," said Susan.

"Why did Grandma and Grandpa hide this from you?"

"Back then, there was more of a stigma associated with adoption. This explains why Grandma was in her forties when she had me though. She had probably tried for years to conceive before that. Maybe she was embarrassed that she couldn't get pregnant." Susan wished she hadn't said that.

"I know what that's like," said Lynette. Susan remembered how difficult it was for Lynette to become pregnant. She and Jason had tried for quite a while before it happened. "Do the papers give the names of your real parents?"

"You mean my birth parents? Grandma and Grandpa will always be my real parents. No, it was a closed adoption."

"Do you want to search for them?" asked Lynette.

"I'm still not sure. I have mixed emotions. On the one hand, it's very difficult for me to squelch my natural curiosity. On the other, I'm afraid of what I might find out. There's a good chance they are no longer even alive. Not everyone lives to be 101 like Grandma did."

The waitress set a heaping plate of chocolate chip pancakes in front of Lynette, and a stack of banana nut pancakes in front of Susan. That first bite tasted like heaven itself.

"Well," said Lynette, "sit with it until you feel comfortable. If you decide to search for them, I'll be happy to help. This is hard to believe. What did Dad think about this?"

Susan poured herself another cup of coffee.

"You know, I haven't even told him yet. He has so much on his mind already. This is a difficult thing for me to talk about. I'll sit down with him and tell him the whole story soon though." Both she and Lynette had attacked their plates with gusto, but both were now beginning to slow down.

"I'm getting stuffed," said Lynette.

"I'll ask for boxes when the waitress comes back. You know, Lynette, I have something to tell you that may be related to the murder case," Susan had decided it was time to share the news about Julie's fake identity.

"What is it, Mom?"

"It's about Julie Martin. She…"

"Owww," cried Lynette. She clutched her stomach and doubled over. "It hurts."

"Lynette, Lynette, what's wrong?" Susan could see that Lynette was in pain and she herself began to panic. She got out of her seat and looked around the restaurant. "Is anyone here a doctor?" she asked.

"Call 911," said Lynette. She clutched Susan's hand. "I think something is terribly wrong. I'm so scared that the baby is in trouble."

Chapter 37

Susan rode in the ambulance with Lynette and called Mike and Jason to tell them what was happening. She was so upset, she wondered if they understood half of what she said. When the ambulance arrived at the hospital, Lynette was quickly taken to the emergency room while Susan paced the floor of the waiting room. She was terrified that her daughter and grandchild were in jeopardy. Soon, Mike and Jason arrived. The nurse took Jason to the back to be with Lynette while Mike stayed with Susan.

"What's going on?" asked Mike. "Is she okay? Is the baby alright?" Mike generally kept his cool during emergencies, but Susan could tell by his voice that he was every bit as worried as she was.

"I don't know anything yet. Everything was just fine. We were enjoying our pancakes when suddenly Lynette doubled over in pain. I called 911 and they came almost immediately. I'm so scared." Mike put his arms around her.

"I'm sure it will be okay. You got her here right away and so far this pregnancy has been smooth sailing. I wish we could do something. I hate that all we can do is wait." Mike went to the vending machine and handed Susan a cup of bitter tasting coffee. He paced back and forth across the room while they waited.

After what seemed like an eternity, Jason came into the waiting room.

"How is she? How's the baby?" asked Susan.

"They are both going to be okay, but the doctor has put Lynette on bed rest. The pain has stopped but they want to keep her here a few hours to make sure."

"Oh, thank God," said Susan. She felt her body relax.

"Jason, we'll be there for you. Susan and I can stay with her while you are at work," said Mike. His strained expression had softened.

"I don't think she will need someone there every minute, but I'm sure she'll appreciate some regular company. The doctor says she has to avoid stress."

"Knowing Lynette, it's going to be hard for her to stay put," said Mike.

"Yes, but I know she'll do everything the doctor says in order to protect the baby," said Jason.

"The important thing is that she stays calm and follows doctor's orders. I'll order up some Netflix, pop some popcorn, and spend my afternoons with her."

"Thanks. We're lucky to have you both nearby. Speaking of which, I need to call my parents and let them know what's going on. Let me go back and do that."

"I'll call you tonight," said Susan. She guessed she would have to explore Julie's past on her own now.

Chapter 38

After the scare with Lynette earlier that day, Susan was having trouble falling asleep. She started thinking about the secrets Julie was keeping. If Julie had faked her own death, then whose identity was she using? Was there a real Julie Martin? If so, where was she? Was she dead? If Julie was capable of keeping her identity a secret for so long, perhaps she wasn't as sweet and naïve as she seemed. Did she have anything to do with the death of the real Julie Martin?

If Zachary posed a threat to her and Joey, that could have been a motive for murder. A mother will go to any lengths to protect her child. If Julie had something to do with the real Julie's death, perhaps Zachary had found out and that would be an even stronger motive. And then there was Tank. Julie seemed like she really cared about him. How could she let him take the blame for a murder she committed?

Susan must have eventually fallen asleep because the next time she looked, the alarm clock said 7:00 and the sun was out. *Mike must be downstairs having breakfast*, she thought. This may be a good time to tell him what I found out about my parents.

"Good morning. I'm glad you finally fell asleep last night. You were tossing and turning something fierce," said Mike. He scooped some scrambled eggs out of the frying pan and put them on a plate. "Do you want some? I can make more."

"No thanks. You have to get to work. I'll sit down with you and have some coffee for now."

"Jason already called this morning. He knows we are early risers. Lynette is doing just fine. At the moment, she's relishing the idea of lounging around in bed all day, but we know her better than that. It won't be long until she starts feeling restless."

"I know, but she will put the baby's wellbeing above everything else. You know that." She swallowed hard. "Mike," she hesitated. "Hey, there's something I want to talk to you about,"

"What is it? You look very serious all of a sudden. I know you've had a lot on your mind these days."

Susan took a deep breath. "I found out something shocking about my parents the other day."

"Shocking? Like what—your mom came from a line of Scottish royalty and abdicated the throne to marry your commoner father?"

"Come on, Mike. Just listen." She went on to tell him how she'd found the adoption papers in the safety deposit box.

"That's unbelievable. Why didn't you tell me sooner? You must have been shocked. Why did you wait this long to tell me?"

"I know. It's just that I needed to get over the initial shock before I could talk about it. And you were so stressed about Tank."

"Did it say in the papers the names of your birth parents?"

"No. It was a closed adoption. I don't even know if the agency still exists and whether or not I even want to pursue this. What if I find out my parents were criminals or something?"

"She was probably an unwed teen. Back in those days it was considered something to be ashamed of, being pregnant and unwed. Lots of times in those cases, parents sent their daughter away somewhere to have the baby, then it was given up for adoption. As far as anyone knew, the girl went on an extended trip to visit relatives or study abroad, then came back home like nothing had ever happened."

"You're probably right. I don't remember watching any Teen Mom reality shows on the three television stations we got when I was a kid, no siree."

"Lynette can probably help you find them. She has time on her hands now. I'll bet she wouldn't mind searching from her laptop or making a few phone calls." Mike grabbed another cup of coffee.

"Not yet. I can't decide what I want to do. I need to think about it a while longer."

"Okay, then. You know I'll support you whatever you decide. Did you tell Lynette yet?"

"Yes. She said she'd help me if I decided I wanted to find them. I'm not sure what the point would be. They may very well be dead or if not, I'm sure they went on to have families of their own. How would their children react to this? It could turn a lot of lives into a tailspin."

"Hey, you might have brothers and sisters running around out there."

"Yeah, I hadn't thought of that. Maybe I'm Angelina Jolie's long lost sister or something."

"Yeah, you look so much alike." Susan gave him a swat. "You know I meant that she would be jealous if she saw how beautiful her older sister was," said Mike. *Boy*, thought Susan. *I have trained this man well.*

"I've got to get to work but we can talk about this some more later. Love ya."

"Love you too," said Susan.

Chapter 39

Dalia was finishing the breakfast she'd ordered from room service when her cell phone began vibrating on the table.

"Oh, hi," said Dalia. "Yes, me too. Things are going so much better now that he's dead. Playing the grieving widow is harder than it seems though. Uh huh. I know. Teamwork. We'll talk again soon."

Dalia ended the call and sat back in her chair. Then she walked over to the dresser drawer and took out Zach's life insurance policy which Phillip had taken from Zach's office safe. Sure enough, she was the sole beneficiary. Good thing he hadn't had time to amend the policy after he realized that his son was still alive. As evil of an oaf as Zach was, he still would have felt an obligation to take care of his son financially. She knew him well enough to be sure of this.

Chapter 40

Susan couldn't shake the feeling that there was more to Julie than met the eye. Even after realizing that she had faked her own death to escape an abusive husband, Susan felt like she was hiding something else. There was obviously a secretive side to Julie, but was there also a sinister one? Could she have pushed Zach into the Jacuzzi and thrown the Boom Box in with him? Maybe knowing more about the real Julie Martin would shed some light on the situation. Was Julie a friend of Kaitlyn's who'd agreed to help her out, or did Kaitlyn kill the real Julie Martin and steal her identity?

She was scheduled to volunteer at the school today and was likely to run into Julie. If so, Susan would have a conversation with her—find out a bit about her life before Westbrook. She pulled on a dark wash pair of trouser jeans and a colorful crew neck sweater, then drove the short distance to the school.

"Hi, Janet. I'm here to help."

"And not a minute too soon," said Janet. "I'm having a heck of a time finding room on the shelves for all these new books that came in. I made a list of some outdated books that we can pull."

"I'll get right to it," said Susan. She got on her knees to start pulling from the bottom shelf when she recognized two familiar voices—Joey and Carolina. She remained hidden from view as they began their conversation.

"Are you doing okay Joey?" asked Carolina.

"Yes. An awful lot has happened in a short period of time, but in the end I'm back where I started. My father is dead. At least, I don't have to go to the police since he's no longer a threat. He would have killed my mother. You heard my mom—he killed Amber accidentally because he was trying to kill my mom. Mom said he'd abused her from the time they were married. We've only been safe these past years because he thought we were dead. As much as I didn't like Amber, she didn't deserve to be killed simply because she was wearing my mom's yellow rain slicker. He had to be stopped."

"I feel so bad for Amber's parents. They must miss her so much. She was an only child too," said Carolina.

"I feel guilty that I dissed her so much. Well, at least in a weird way, justice was served. Her killer is dead."

"Come on, here's the book I need to check out. Let's do that and get to class before we're late." Carolina and Joey left the library just as Julie came in.

I wonder if Joey had it in him to kill Zach. After all, he had that paper under his bed with Amber's name on it. And now his hand was bandaged. She hadn't noticed that at the shower. Maybe he isn't the golden boy he appears to be, thought Susan. She got up and walked over to Julie.

"That was a beautiful shower you gave Lynette," said Julie. "It's too bad that you had to find a dead body in the Jacuzzi the next morning—that must have been horrible—but aside from that, Lynette will always remember that night." Susan was stuck by how nonchalant Julie's tone was. She would have expected her to sound sad, angry—some kind of emotion when talking about the dead body.

"Thanks. Did your parents throw you a shower when you were expecting Joey? Did they live near you back then?" asked Susan.

"My parents were in New Jersey, but, no, they didn't. Actually, my coworkers did."

"Schoolteachers throw good parties. I'll bet it was great." Susan watched closely for a reaction.

Julie told her that she'd been a paralegal back then.

"It was a lifetime ago." Julie looked at her watch. "Got to get back to work."

As Susan watched Julie leave, she couldn't help wondering why she would have given up her paralegal career for a teaching job. *Unless the real Julie Martin was a teacher,* thought Susan. That might be an avenue to explore. Susan sat at a vacant computer and looked at the New Jersey Department of Education website. She knew it was possible to look up a particular teacher's license and areas of certification. Nothing came up under the New Jersey site. *Maybe she lived nearby in New York,* thought Susan. *Susan knew lots of people who worked in the city but lived in New Jersey or even Connecticut.*

When she tried the New York State Department of Education site, she hit pay dirt. Julie Martin had received a teaching certificate in 1999. *But this is weird* thought Susan. If Julie was still working as a paralegal in 1999, she must not have had a teaching license yet. Stranger still, the certificate had been renewed two years ago. This Julie was working using the real Julie Martin's teaching license.

Susan left the school and decided to check up on Lynette—and perhaps get her help. She picked up food along the way.

"Hi, Mom. Mmm, you got it. I smell egg rolls," said Lynette.

Susan handed her two paper bags. "Eggs rolls, and Baskin Robbins' Quarterback Crunch ice cream."

"You're the best. Want some?"

"No thanks. I'm trying to be good. Dad has lost close to ten pounds already and I've gained two or three. I'll sit with you though." Susan poured herself a glass of water from the tap and brought a plate and eating utensils to the dining room table.

"Lynette, I don't want to stress you out with police matters, but I could use your help. I found out some things regarding Zach's murder."

"Mom, I'm so bored that I won't even chastise you for sleuthing without a license. Tell me."

"Well, first of all, Julie Martin was once married to Zach. He was an abusive husband. Julie somehow faked her own death and moved here with Joey fifteen years ago.

Zach found out that she was still alive and came here after her."

"Mom, are you sure? How could you possibly know this?"

"I overheard a conversation the night of the shower. I wasn't trying to eavesdrop mind you. I just happened to be standing behind that giant oak we have when Julie and Dalia began talking."

"I didn't realize they knew each other. We interviewed Julie. She never mentioned that she even knew Zach."

"I was surprised, but boy, I got an earful. Dalia had figured out that Zach's first wife was still alive and that he had come to Westbrook to harm her. She had figured out that Julie was Zach's first wife and must have told this to Julie sometime earlier.

"That's incredible. We questioned everyone who was at the shower that night but we had no reason to suspect Dalia or Julie. How did I miss that? How does this tie in with Zach killing Amber though? We still haven't uncovered a motive."

"Zach had been following Julie. One night she was wearing a yellow rain slicker. When Zach came to the school that night, he saw a woman in a yellow rain slicker leaving out of the back door of Julie's classroom. Amber was following the path Julie normally took to walk home. He was trying to kill Julie, but killed Amber by mistake."

"Oh my God, that's awful." Lynette shook her head. "I don't know how to even begin explaining that one to Amber's parents. She was killed by mistake? How horrible is that?"

"I know. Well, at least we have a motive. In some way maybe that will help give closure to the Bernsteins."

"Mom, why didn't you tell me this sooner?" Susan hated when Lynette used that scolding parent tone on her.

"I didn't want to upset you. I was starting to tell you at IHop the day you wound up in the emergency room," said Susan. "Another thing. I was curious about the real Julie Martin so I searched and found that she was a teacher in

New York. She had gotten her license in 1999. At that time, our Julie was working as a paralegal. I think she assumed Julie's identity and her profession."

"Boy, you've been busy. If that's true, the real Julie Martin is probably dead. They must have known each other."

"I know. And maybe Julie even killed the real Julie so she could escape Zach and even have a way of supporting herself and her son."

"Now that's a bit of a leap, even for you Mom."

"In any case, I'm thinking that if we can maybe find Julie's parents, we can find out what happened to her and whether or not she and our Julie were friends. Problem is, I need a real detective to help me find them." Susan looked at Lynette with pleading eyes.

"Oh, this is so against my better judgment." She thought about it for a few minutes. "I can't very well go and do it myself though." She patted her stomach. Susan could practically see the wheels turning inside her daughter's head. "Okay. I'll look into it for you. I'd ask Jackson to investigate this, but he wouldn't be happy that we are basing all this on a conversation my Mom heard while standing behind an oak tree at my baby shower."

"Yeah. I guess that sounds a little ridiculous."

"I'll get back to you when I find something. Then we will bring Julie and Dalia in for questioning. That's one giant motive. They are both primary suspects now."

"Oh, and one more thing."

"There's more?" Lynette emphasized the word *more*.

"Yes. Joey apparently heard the conversation also. I heard him talking to Carolina about it at the school media center."

"Mom....really?"

"Anyhow, he was piping mad about his father surfacing and worried about his mother. He may have pushed Zach into that Jacuzzi to protect her. He has a temper—I've seen it myself. And he's sporting a bandage on his right hand.

Maybe he injured himself while pushing Zach into the Jacuzzi."

"I guess that gives us three prime suspects then. Good work, Mom." Susan couldn't believe Lynette actually said those words to her but she'd graciously accept the compliment.

Chapter 41

The next day, Lynette called with a home address and phone number for Julie Martin's parents. They lived in Westchester County, only about an hour or so away. Susan debated calling them, but decided to jump into her Prius and drive there instead. It would be harder to close a door in someone's face than it would be to simply hang up on them. That was her reasoning anyway. She came to an affluent neighborhood and soon found the house. She was nervous but anxious as she knocked on the door.

"Hello, Mrs. Martin? My name is Susan Wiles. I'm a friend of an old friend of your daughter." Mrs. Martin appeared understandably puzzled.

"Then you know my Julie has been dead since 2001. What brings you here now? What friend?" Understandably, she sounded suspicious.

"Her name is Kaitlyn Chichester," said Susan. "I think maybe they worked together."

"Come on in." Susan followed Mrs. Martin into the living room.

"That name doesn't sound familiar. It's been a while now though. Sometimes I have to remind myself that it's been fifteen years. It seems like yesterday."

"I can imagine. I understand Julie was a teacher. Do you think Kaitlyn may have been a colleague?"

"If you're a friend of Kaitlyn's, you should know the answer to that. Why didn't you ask her?" said Mrs. Martin.

Susan sensed that this conversation was about to end. She fidgeted on the couch as she summoned her creative muse. *Think, Susan, think,* she told herself. "Well, the thing is, Kaitlyn has gone missing and we're looking for clues to her whereabouts. The first 24 hours are crucial you know. We found a picture in her apartment of her and Julie. It had a caption on the back." Susan was at the same time ashamed and proud of herself for being able to conjure up a plausible story under pressure.

"Oh my. If this Kaitlyn was able to escape from the towers, only to go missing fifteen years later, what a shame. Her poor parents must be beside themselves."

"The towers?" *Did she hear her correctly?* "What do you mean?" asked Susan. She replayed the words inside of her head, trying to comprehend them.

"911. Julie died during the 911 attack. She worked in one of the towers."

"I'm so awfully sorry." Susan swallowed and tried to digest this shocking piece of information.

"Thanks. It doesn't get any easier. People say it does with time but the more time passes, the longer it's been since I've been able to hear her voice or give her a hug. I miss her so much."

"That has to be horrible. I can't imagine losing a child like that. My mom died recently. That's difficult enough but at least she had had a chance to live out her life."

"The worst thing is that they never even found her remains. The explosion was so forceful, they say two out of three bodies were beyond being able to identify. We had a memorial service but it's not the same as putting her to rest with a proper burial. I feel like I never got to say goodbye."

"What did your daughter do at the twin towers?"

"She worked in the daycare. She had gotten her license and was looking for a teaching job, but meanwhile she was supporting herself by teaching a preschool class there. She loved being with the kids. She was great with kids."

"Again, what a terrible loss, so senseless. Thank you for taking the time to speak with me. I should be going." Susan got up and walked toward the door.

"I'm sorry I couldn't be of more help. I hope you find your friend safe and sound."

"Me too."

Chapter 42

As soon as she was on the road, Susan called Lynette to tell her what she'd learned. Lynette was as shocked as she was. Lynette agreed that it may have been possible for Kaitlyn to allow herself to be assumed dead and to steal Julie's identity *if* she happened to be working in the towers at the time of the explosion.

"Mom, I will have to confirm that Kaitlyn was working in the twin towers on 911. Even if she was there that day and managed to escape, it still leaves me to wonder how she would have had access to Julie's identity. After all, Kaitlyn couldn't simply have applied for a driver's license or a copy of Julie's teaching certificate without proper identification."

"I'll have to think about that one," said Susan. "The other thing is Joey. If he attended the preschool, wouldn't he have, in all probability, died along with the real Julie? They would have been at the same place. Even if he had survived, how would Kaitlyn possibly have gotten to him in all the chaos and confusion?"

"Remember, this is all conjecture. There are lots of unanswered questions. First things first. I'll call you back when I confirm that Kaitlyn was working in the twin towers during that time."

"Okay, Lynette. Get some rest and take care of my grandbaby."

"Will do, Deputy Mom."

Susan decided to stop off and see Dalia on her way home. After all, Dalia had no one here in Westbrook. She was stuck here waiting for Zach's body to be released and was probably going crazy waiting. Grieving is hard enough. She ached every day, missing her mom. But to grieve with no family or friends around? That must be unbearable. She pulled into Rocking Horse Ranch, took the elevator to Dalia's floor, and made her way to the room. As she was about to knock, she heard voices. Dalia was talking to someone. They were laughing, actually. Dalia didn't seem to be grieving at all.

"Come home with me. I miss you." It was a man's voice.

"Phillip, are you nuts? I'm supposed to be a grieving widow. It will look fishy if I leave Zach in Westbrook while I go back to New Jersey with my dead husband's business partner. We have to be smart about this." Susan realized that it was Zach's business partner (and obviously, Dalia's lover) who Dalia was talking to. Just when she was convincing herself that Julie...she meant Kaitlyn...was the murderer, Dalia was sounding awfully suspicious.

"I know you're right, but it's been hard waiting like this. I want us to be a family—me, you, and our baby." *It could have even been Phillip,* thought Susan. *Oh wait, he supposedly had an alibi. How careful had the police been in confirming that?*

Susan was startled by the sound of a door slamming shut down the hall. She rummaged through her purse, pretending to look for her keycard while one of the legitimate hotel guests passed by. Then, back to the task at hand. She pressed her ear right up against the door.

"We will be together, but we need to be careful," said Dalia. "Go on back home to the office and keep the business afloat while we wait this out."

Susan jumped as she heard the cleaning cart being wheeled down the hallway. She quickly extricated her ear from the door and walked toward the elevator as if she was a guest going downstairs for a bite to eat. She wanted to go back and hear more of the conversation, but in reality she'd gotten the gist of things. She wanted to tell Lynette right away how happy they'd seemed, but was worried. Lynette had been surprisingly willing to let her talk to Julie's family, but knowing her mom was eavesdropping–

–again—might try Lynette's patience. Besides, Lynette had this thing about Susan putting herself into dangerous situations. Susan had almost gotten killed last winter while solving the Vicky Roger's murder case, but heck, she was like her cats Ludwig and Johann—she had nine lives. She had solved the case and come out of it unscathed.

Chapter 43

Boy, sleuthing makes me hungry, thought Susan. She could go straight home and make herself a salad, or she could take a detour through the McDonald's drive-thru. All that anxiety about being caught outside Dalia's door surely had burned some serious calories.

Susan had no sooner changed into comfortable clothes and planted herself in front of the Dr. Oz show, when Lynette called to confirm that Kaitlyn had been working for a legal firm in the twin towers during 2001. Her son Joey had been registered with the daycare. It seemed unlikely that Kaitlyn had had anything to do with Julie's death. It looked as if she'd simply seized an opportunity. Susan ran through the state of the investigation. Dalia was being abused by Zach, was pregnant, and was involved with Zach's business partner, Phillip. She could have smothered Zach with a pillow or put antifreeze in his Gatorade any given day. Why would she choose to murder Zach at the baby shower where she'd risk being seen?

Phillip had motive to kill Zach because he wanted to be with Dalia and if Zach were dead, he and Dalia would own the company. Then there was the life insurance—like on *Dateline*. Surely Dalia was the beneficiary of that life insurance policy. He and Dalia would be set financially—unless another wife or a son turned up. Phillip had an alibi though. He was at the Chamber of Commerce banquet in New Jersey, presenting one of the awards the night of the murder.

Julie, of course, wanted to protect herself and her son from the dangerous husband she'd escaped from fifteen years ago. Joey, whose temper and strength Susan had witnessed with her own eyes, had just found out that his father was alive, and that he had tried to kill his mother. To top it off, his newly discovered father had killed Amber, an innocent girl, because he mistook her for his mom. Either he or his mother could have killed in a fit of rage that night. They both had been at the shower. They both had had the opportunity.

Then there was Mr. Bernstein. Zach had killed his daughter because he had mistaken her for Julie. Mr. Bernstein surely had motive, but he was a lawyer and had just uncovered evidence that would have had Zach locked up in jail for the remainder of his life. He was an intelligent man and Susan was inclined to think that he was too rational to have killed Zach in a rage. He did admit to being at the scene though. And he had just discovered that Zach was his daughter's killer hours earlier.

And no one had even considered Mrs. Bernstein. She acted very confused when Susan and Lynette ran into the Bernsteins outside of *Babies and Such*. She had appeared to have been heavily drugged. Could she have followed her husband to our house that night and killed Zach after learning from him that Zach was her daughter's killer? Drugs could mess with rational thinking. So could having your daughter murdered.

Susan needed to clear her head. She had never completely finished cleaning up the yard after the baby shower. The wind had been strong the past few days and there were fragments of streamers and deflated balloons all the way in the neighbors' back yard. Susan grabbed a Hefty garbage bag and began crisscrossing the yard, picking up remnants of shower decorations. She started close to the Jacuzzi, although the crime scene investigators seemed to have done quite a thorough job. The area closest to the Jacuzzi was still blocked with yellow crime scene tape. When she had worked her way outward onto the neighbor's property, she bent down to grab a piece of pink streamer and next to it found a weathered paper that appeared to be some sort of receipt. *I wonder what this is from?* she thought.

She examined the receipt, thinking it had most likely dropped out of the neighbor's purse. It was stiffer than an ordinary receipt, and had what appeared to be the name of a business, and a series of numbers. She stuck it into the pocket of her sweat jacket, finished her canvas of the extended crime scene, and went back inside. Mike would be coming home soon. Maybe he'd recognize the name of the company.

Chapter 44

No sooner had Susan locked the sliding glass door behind her than she heard Mike's car in the driveway.

"Hey, Hon. How was your day?" asked Susan. She was anxious to show him the receipt.

"Pretty quiet. I'm starving. What's for dinner?"

"I was going to broil some seasoned chicken breasts and toss a salad."

"What did you do today?" asked Mike.

"I was busy. I spent some time with Lynette. I'm helping her with the murder case." Mike raised an eyebrow. "No, really. I found the real Julie Martin's mother. Get this, her daughter was killed during the twin towers' attack. She worked at the daycare. Kaitlyn—that's the woman we've been calling Julie—was working there as a paralegal in a law office. They had to have known each other."

"Run that by me again? On second thought, never mind. If they worked on different floors, how could Kaitlyn have known that Julie died? And if Julie had been killed in the explosion, how is it that her purse wouldn't have been destroyed?"

"You know, Joey had been enrolled in the daycare. That has to be the connection. Somehow these pieces must fit together." Susan suddenly remembered the receipt she had found outside. "Mike, I found this in the yard."

Mike took the receipt and looked it over carefully. "Starlight Express. You know, I've heard of that. I think it's a valet company. They park cars during events. Why would it have been in our yard? We certainly didn't have valet parking the night of the shower and I didn't notice our neighbors throwing any big bashes lately—or ever come to think of it."

"A valet company? It had to have dropped out of someone's pocket."

Mike looked at the ticket again. "It's dated the same night as the shower. It doesn't have a city on it though. You should run this by Lynette."

"I'll take it over to her first thing in the morning."

Chapter 45

Susan knew that Lynette had asked Jackson to go back and re-interview all the guests who'd attended the shower. He had found witnesses who were able to confirm that Zach was still alive when both Julie and Dalia left the patio. Even though Dalia and Zach had taken separate cars to the shower, Susan still thought it was a little strange how Dalia didn't notice that Zach never came home from the shower. Then again, according to Julie, Zach was a psychopath and Susan herself had seen how poorly he treated Dalia. Maybe they weren't in the habit of spending their nights together anymore. Besides, Dalia was pregnant. Susan remembered how tired she'd been during her pregnancies, so maybe Dalia had just fallen into a deep sleep.

"Come on," said Mike. "Get out of bed and let's go on our walk. Pretty soon it will be too cold in the mornings."

"Okay, I'm coming." Susan nudged Ludwig so she could get out of bed, then threw on a pair of sweats. It was refreshingly chilly outside.

"Do you think they're closing in on Zach's murderer?" asked Mike.

"Well, they've pretty much cleared Julie and Dalia. Phillip, Zach's business partner, has an alibi. He was presenting at an awards ceremony in New Jersey that night. That leaves Joey and Amber's father—or her mother. Joey had his hand bandaged the other day at school. It wasn't wrapped up the night of the party. Do you think he might have injured it pushing Zach into the Jacuzzi?"

"No, it wouldn't have taken a lot of force if Zach was caught off-guard at the edge of the Jacuzzi. Besides,

Lynette said there was no sign of a struggle. Did you ask him what happened? "

"I did, but he kind of made a joke out of it. We could take a careful look around the patio. If he injured it at the shower maybe there are traces of blood."

Mike reminded her that the police had gone over the area with a fine-toothed comb. It was unlikely that they would have missed blood. Of course, Susan wouldn't be satisfied until she looked for herself. After all, they had missed the valet ticket.

"Susan, I just had a thought. Of all the suspects you've mentioned, who would most likely have used valet parking?"

"I'd say Zach's business partner, but he had witnesses who saw him at the ceremony."

"Just suppose he left the ceremony early. It's possible that he could have driven up from New Jersey. It's not that far."

"I don't know. How long do you think it takes to drive from there to here?"

"I'd say he could do it in under two hours."

"How about if I spend the day researching the event and after work, you and I can take a little field trip. We could even stop for dinner on the way back. We'll drive right by Amici's."

"I know there's no point in arguing. Yes, let's do it. I'll try to leave work a little early," said Mike. "Wear that sexy black number of yours. And don't forget your Pandora bracelet with the sleuth charm that I gave you for your birthday. On second thought, how about you wear *only* the Pandora bracelet?"

"You got it, big guy." Sleuthing was more and more fun all the time.

After Mike left for work, Susan began researching business award ceremonies and after a bit of surfing, she found one that had taken place the night of the murder. That ceremony had started at seven pm. She found a program on-line. Phillip had been the very first presenter.

But there were witnesses who placed him there thought Susan. She wrote down the name of the hotel and used MapQuest to get directions. This way they'd be ready to go as soon as Mike got home.

Then she took a long, relaxing shower and wiggled into the black dress Mike was talking about. It felt tighter than last time she'd worn it. How was that possible? After all, she'd been dieting and exercising for a few months already. Well, she'd spent more than a few afternoons watching movies and eating ice cream over at Lynette's. She looked at herself in the mirror. *So this is what they mean by batwings,* she thought. *I think I'll grab my black sweater. After all, it will probably be cold in the restaurant.*

"Hey, I'm home," called Mike. He took a few minutes to change and they were on their way. "Write down our start time," he said when they got into the car. Susan read the directions as he drove. Mike didn't officially speed, but he tried to hustle since he knew Phillip would have been in a rush. They arrived at the hotel one hour and forty minutes later.

"Well, it's possible that he could have presented the award, collected his car from valet parking, and gotten to the baby shower in time to kill Zach," said Susan.

"What do you think his motive would have been?"

"Mike, he was carrying on with Zach's wife and she's expecting a baby. It could very well be his baby. He probably knew that Zach was an abusive husband. And then there's the fact that Zach was driving the business into the toilet."

"That could be it."

"Now, if we could only prove that he left the ceremony early. She scanned the parking lot. Hmmm, that looks like valet parking over at that entrance. And look, it's the same company—Starlight. I'll bet the hotel uses the same service for all its events. What do you say we talk to the guys doing the parking?"

"That's a stretch. I don't know…"

"Come on. We're here. We might as well try. Drive over there." Susan got out of the car and started talking to the valet before Mike had even turned off the car. The attendant walked around to the driver's side to get the keys.

"No thank you, sir," said Susan. "We're not staying. We were just wondering if you would help us out with something. Do you mind if I ask you a few questions?" The attendant shrugged his shoulders. Susan took this as an invitation to proceed. "Were you working here the night of October 22?"

"Miss, how do you expect me to remember? My schedule changes every week. I can barely remember what I ate for lunch—or if I even ate lunch."

"Please try. It's important. Our son told his wife that he was here at an awards ceremony that night. She thinks he was having a tryst with his secretary. Their marriage depends on proving that he was really here that night. And they're expecting a baby. You don't want to see some poor innocent baby be born into a broken family, now do you?" *Thank you creative muse,* thought Susan. Mike gave her a look and shook his head. Just then, another valet walked back from parking a Porsche. He had overheard the conversation.

"Miss, are you talking about the Chamber of Commerce awards? I was working that night. I only remember because I was supposed to be off, but my girlfriend had this Halloween party she wanted to go to so I switched days with my buddy Mario."

"Oh, please tell me you can help me. Did you notice anyone leaving soon after the event began? Someone who may have been in a hurry? Think hard." Susan's heart started beating faster.

The valet took a few minutes to think before answering. "I can't believe I remember this, but yes, one guy came out right after the event started. I had just parked his vintage Mercedes and now he wanted me to retrieve it. Seemed to be in a big hurry. He peeled out of here as soon as I brought it to him."

"What did he look like? Was he in his forties, brown hair, tall and thin?"

"That sounds like him. Must have been a smoker. That beautiful car smelled like a bar on steroids."

"Thank you so much," said Susan. As soon as they had the car to themselves, Susan shrieked, "We did it. We solved the case. It must have been Phillip who killed Zach."

Mike gave her a high five. "This isn't definitive proof, although that parking attendant blows a hole in Phillip's alibi. Let's call Lynette right away."

"Well, not right away. She's probably asleep anyway. Don't we have a dinner date?" She pulled down the V-necked dress to show a little more cleavage.

"You got it," said Mike. "First things first."

Chapter 46

The next morning, Susan took the valet parking receipt to Lynette and told her what she and Mike had discovered. Lynette agreed to have Jackson drive to the hotel and take a statement from the valet. Then he would once again question Phillip. Lynette was cautious as always, but Susan could tell that she thought this could prove Phillip was the killer. Susan headed to the school to volunteer for a few hours.

On the way to the school, Susan plotted her actions. She would try to talk to Julie, and perhaps get her to open up about the twin towers. *That would be like prying food from a dog's mouth,* she thought, but, nonetheless, she could try. She couldn't leave that mystery unsolved. When she entered the media center, she found Janet overwhelmed as usual.

"So glad to see you," said Janet. "I'm trying to sort through all these VHS tapes. We're replacing all the VCR's with DVD players as they wear out, but some of the tapes are worth keeping, at least for now."

"I'll grab this pile," said Susan. She chatted with Janet until Julie/Kaitlyn came in as usual during her planning period. Julie/Kaitlyn asked Susan about Lynette.

"She's doing well, staying off her feet like the doctor ordered. She's getting a bit stir crazy, but she'd do anything to protect that baby."

"Glad to hear she's doing well."

"Julie, can we go somewhere private to talk?" asked Susan.

Julie raised an eyebrow. "Sure, I guess so. Come on back to my classroom." Susan followed her to a room a few doors from the media center. "What's going on?"

Again, Susan channeled her creative muse. "I think I need to share something with you. I heard Lynette talking to her partner on the phone. She said that she'd discovered a link between you and Zach. She said you'd once been married to him. I'm just telling you this because you're my friend and I don't want you to be blindsided when the police question you about it. They may be thinking you had motive to kill Zach, and you certainly had the opportunity the night of the shower. I mean, I know you could never kill someone, but the police might consider you a suspect." Julie's shoulders dropped and Susan watched the color drain from her face. It took her a moment to respond.

"Susan," she spoke slowly and deliberately, "This is terrible. I never wanted to have to admit this. Yes, I was married to Zach once, but I didn't kill him. It's going to look bad if the police start digging into this though."

"Why's that? Lots of couples divorce and that's not usually motive for murder."

"Yes, but…"

"But what? You can tell me. I want to help. I'm on your side."

"We were never divorced. Zach was an abusive husband, both physically and emotionally. He gave me this scar on my wrist, for example, by holding my wrist down on the stove burner. He was a horrible and dangerous man."

"That's terrible. I'm glad you got away from him."

"Oh, getting away was not an easy task. I knew that if I left or threatened divorce he would have killed me. He never would have let me go. When Joey was born, I was terrified that he would start hurting him too."

"And did he?" asked Susan.

"Not at first. It started around the time that Joey turned four. It broke my heart. I didn't know where to turn. Zach was a very influential man in our community. He had connections. If he didn't kill me, he would have certainly taken Joey away from me. I never would have seen my son again." Julie's cheeks were wet with tears.

"So how did you manage to escape?"

"An unexpected opportunity fell into my lap on the tail of one of this country's worst tragedies. One day, as I was commuting to work, Joey started crying hysterically. We took the train every morning into Manhattan. There was an onsite daycare/preschool at my work. He'd been a little fussy that morning, but now he seemed to be in pain and he felt warm. By the time I got off the train, I knew he was sick."

"So what did you do?" asked Susan. She leaned forward.

"Joey had this wonderful preschool teacher. Her name was Julie Martin. When I got to the daycare, she could see that Joey was sick. She offered to let me take her car to run him over to the pediatrician. She was so goodhearted like that. So I took her up on the offer and drove him to the pediatrician. Turns out he had an ear infection. On the way back, I heard the most horrifying news on the radio. The Twin Towers had been attacked. My head was spinning. Then it sunk in. I was supposed to have been there that morning. Joey was supposed to be at the daycare. It was a miracle that we weren't. I couldn't wrap my head around it."

"Wow, talk about luck."

"Yeah, a little divine intervention maybe. Anyhow, when I heard the news, I just froze. I pulled into a parking lot and just sat there. I knew they weren't letting cars anywhere near the towers. I was shaking, thinking about my coworkers and Julie. I thought about the poor kids at the daycare and prayed they had escaped. I couldn't stop crying. I must have sat there for hours. Joey had fallen asleep in the back. Then it occurred to me. I was supposed to be there. Not a soul besides Julie knew that I had taken Joey to the doctor. I wondered if I could maybe just take Joey and disappear. Zach would think we had died in the explosion and wouldn't try to find us. It seemed like the perfect solution."

"Where did you go?" asked Susan.

"My parents have been living abroad for many years. Before they left the states, they owned a small house here in Westbrook which they rented out during the summers. They still own it. It was fall so the summer renters had already left. I knew I could stay there for a while."

"That was brave of you." Susan couldn't believe how lucky Julie had been. She tried to piece it together. "How did you have money to live on?"

"I had a secret bank account. I'd been stashing away small amounts of money for years. I was planning on running away from Zach one day. I just hadn't gotten up the courage. I also had Julie's car and—call it divine intervention—but she'd left her gym bag with her wallet inside it in the trunk. I was sick about Julie, but somehow I knew she would have been okay with what I did."

"How did you know that Julie hadn't escaped?"

"I waited weeks, then months, to hear news but they never found her remains. If she were alive, I would have heard. Besides, the daycare was hit hard, there weren't many survivors."

"You must have been scared being in a new town with a small child like that. Didn't the money eventually run out?" asked Susan. She imagined how alone and scared Julie must have felt.

"Remember, I had Julie's driver's license and credit cards. Her social security card was even there in her wallet. I started to wonder if just maybe I could get away with becoming her. She had a teaching certificate. I applied at the school district to substitute and started getting called. Eventually I was offered a full time position and here I am."

"How did Zach find you then after all these years? You must have been terrified."

"Zach had seen us on *Sixty Minutes* when they did that story about Joey winning the national science contest. I told you he had connections. It didn't take him long to hunt us down."

"Julie, I have to ask. Did you push him into the Jacuzzi the night of the shower? I'm sure you felt threatened. I'd understand if you did."

"No, Susan. Of course not. I don't have it in me to commit murder even considering how much I hated Zach. We argued on the patio that night, but he was alive the last time I saw him."

"Julie, you need to go to the police with this before they come to you."

"Oh God, I don't know if I can. I don't want to go to jail. What would happen to Joey then?"

"Just tell them the whole story. I'm sure they're going to find the real killer soon."

"Let me call downstairs and see if I can get a sub. I'm in no position to teach today. Then I'll go over to the station."

"Ask for Jackson Simpson. He's Lynette's partner. He was at the shower."

"Okay, I'll summon up my courage and do that."

"Call me if you need anything." Susan was still absorbing the enormity of the situation as she exited the school. She felt in her heart that Julie couldn't have killed Zach, and she had faith that the Westbrook Police Department would find the real killer soon. She was convinced that Phillip was the murderer. She walked through a crowd of students eating lunch at the picnic tables outside the school and heard a familiar hello. It was Carolina.

"Hey, Mrs. W.! Volunteering today?" asked Carolina. She was with Joey Martin. Susan wondered if the two of them were an official couple or just good friends.

"Good to see you, sweetie. How's your dad? He looked great at the shower."

"He's good. We've come to a new normal since Mom died. I still miss her though."

"I'm sure you will always miss her." Susan thought about her own birth mother and wondered if she ever missed the daughter she gave up. "Joey, what happened to your hand?" asked Susan. His right hand was still bandaged and wrapped.

"Oh, just a little run in with a cement wall," said Joey. Susan wondered if by cement wall he was referring to the garden wall in back of her house. Joey was in a hurry, but Carolina stayed back for a few minutes.

"Carolina, seriously, how did Joey injure his hand?"

"He was telling the truth. You know he has a temper when he gets angry or frustrated. Something had upset him at the baby shower. He hauled off and punched the back wall of your house."

"Seriously? What was it that had him so upset?"

Carolina looked down at the floor and hesitated. "I really can't say. You'll have to ask Joey. I'd better run too now or I'll be late to class."

Susan said goodbye. Even though it looked as if Phillip was the murderer, they still hadn't gotten back the DNA report. They'd taken DNA samples from all the suspects, but processing DNA took time. She set off for home, wondering again if Joey was at all capable of murder.

Chapter 47

Jackson Simpson was eating his lunch at the station when Julie came in. She told him the whole story about the Twin Towers and how she had assumed the real Julie Martin's identity. Jackson reassured her that she wouldn't be facing jail time, at least not for that crime.

"Did anyone see you on the patio or going inside the house while Mr. Chichester was still alive?" asked Jackson.

"Dalia Chichester saw me. So did Tank Copland. As a matter of fact, I'm sure Dalia was still outside when I came in." Her account pretty much matched what the witnesses he had interviewed told him. He would reconfirm the statements he had taken, but it looked as if Julie/Kaitlyn would be cleared.

Julie left the station. Jackson resumed eating his sandwich and chips, licking the orange barbecue powder off of his fingers. Lynette used to hate it when he did that. She used to tell him that it was as bad as listening to someone crack their knuckles, another thing she hated. When he finished, he called Dalia Chichester and asked her to come in. Then he resumed working.

"Hi, honey." Theresa Rizzo walked into the station. Jackson's heart still fluttered every time he heard her voice. "I was on the way home from school and thought I'd stop by and bring you a present. The chorus was having a bake sale today. I bought you some brownies." She shook the bag in front of his nose. Theresa taught fourth grade at Westchester Elementary.

"A woman after my own heart," said Jackson. He peeked into the bag and licked his lips. He couldn't wait to propose to Theresa, as soon as he could come up with a plan. It had to be special, something memorable. He had already bought her a ring and imagined a thousand times in his mind how it would feel to slip it on her finger.

"The kids were crazy today," said Theresa. "We had an assembly in the morning and they were riled up for the whole day. I hate when they bring in those fundraising people who offer them cheap prizes for selling magazines, all in the name of raising money for the school."

While they were talking, Dalia Chichester walked in. Jackson told Theresa to wait while he took Dalia into a conference room. Dalia confirmed that she had seen Julie leave the patio while Zach was still alive and she swore that Zach was still alive when she herself had come back into the house.

"Thank you for your cooperation," said Jackson. He walked her to the front entrance and then sat down next to Theresa. "Well, Dalia Chichester confirmed that one of our suspects has an alibi. Now we need to clear her."

"Jacky, this is your lucky day. I talked to Dalia at the shower. I went outside for a few minutes to get some air and I started talking to her. We were talking shoes. Anyhow, that big mouth Zach was there. It sounded like he was shouting, he had such a big, booming voice. I saw Julie Martin talking to him, then she went inside. A few minutes later, Dalia said she was getting cold and we both came back in. Zach was still talking to someone else outside, so I know he was alive at that point."

"Did you see who he was talking to?" asked Jackson. He raised an eyebrow.

"No, but it was a man. I heard a man's voice."

"A man or a young man? Joey Martin was there that night. He's on our suspect list."

"It was definitely an older voice, and I didn't see Joey outside at all."

"Well, Theresa, you just cleared Dalia. That's very helpful." He gave her a kiss.

"Glad I could help. You should have asked me earlier. We're still on for tonight, right?"

"You bet. I'll pick you up at six." Jackson couldn't wait. Tonight was going to be *the* night. He'd made up his mind. "Oh, and take this." He handed her a small branch.

"Jacky, what on earth is this?" said Theresa.

"Oh, just a little gift. Go with it. See you tonight."

Chapter 48

Susan was thinking about her mother a lot these days. She decided to stop at the cemetery. The ground was still fresh and the headstone wasn't ready yet, but, nonetheless, it was a comfort being near her mom. She told her about Lynette's shower and how she'd helped decorate the baby's room. Her heart ached. Her mother would have been so thrilled to have a great grandchild. It was starting to drizzle, so Susan headed toward the car. Along the path, she recognized a familiar face. It was Mrs. Bernstein at Amber's grave. She walked quietly so as not to disturb her. As she got nearer, she could tell Mrs. Bernstein was talking to her dead daughter.

"Amber, I miss you so much. To think you died because that Zachary Chichester mistook you for his former wife. I...we couldn't let him get away with that." Susan could hear sobbing between the words.

She crouched down behind a neighboring gravestone. *This could be very interesting. Was Amber's mother saying she had something to do with Zach's death?*

"My baby. You know I couldn't imagine anyone hating you enough to kill you. When I heard Daddy saying that a stranger, some Zachary something or other, had killed you I felt an explosion inside my head. He was not going to get away with it."

Was this a confession? thought Susan. She heard voices behind her. She was no longer alone on the path and didn't want to be caught crouching behind a gravestone, eavesdropping, so she got up (reminded again about how she needed some yoga classes) and walked back to the car. Just when it was looking like a slam dunk that Phillip was the killer, here was yet another possibility.

Chapter 49

Jackson took a second shower, dabbed on some Old Spice, and combed what was left of his hair. He was fidgeting and had already checked his pocket three times to make sure the ring was still there. He picked up Theresa promptly at six.

"Wow, you look stunning," he said to Theresa as she opened the door. She was wearing a short beaded dress and carried a matching purse. Jackson purposely inhaled. He loved the vanilla-scented perfume she always wore.

"You too, handsome." Theresa followed Jackson to the car. Theresa got into the car and sat on something small and hard.

"Ouch, what's this?" she said. She pulled a plastic, magnetic letter U from under her bottom.

"Oh, just go with it," said Jackson. He was enjoying this and broke into a grin. He pulled into Kenny Tang's.

"Asian Fusion? So you're finally willing to try this place?" said Theresa. Jackson wasn't much for trying new things. Theresa had suggested this place multiple times, but they'd always wound up at Vinnie's or Amici's.

"Yep, I'm taking the plunge," said Jackson. His stomach felt like a wave pool inside. He didn't know if he could eat. They followed the hostess to a candle-lit table in the corner. The waitress approached them.

"Good evening. My name is Mary. I'll be your server tonight." She poured them a complimentary glass of house wine. Theresa looked more beautiful than ever in the glow of the candlelight. They had a delicious stir-fried dinner and decided to top it off with dessert.

"How about we share the green tea ice cream with almond cookies?" suggested Jackson.

"Sounds good to me," agreed Theresa. The dessert arrived and Theresa said, "Jacky, why is there an M on this almond cookie and an E on this one? That's really strange."

"Well, my love. It seems that it spells out a word." He felt his heart beat accelerating. His hands were sweating.

"*Me*. Why does it say that?" asked Theresa.

"Okay, you've been a detective's girlfriend long enough to be able to put together simple clues. What odd gifts did you receive today?" asked Jackson.

Theresa thought for a moment. "Well, you handed me a leafless branch at the station."

"What was it made of?"

"Wood. It was made of wood."

"Next?"

"In the car I sat on the magnetic letter U."

"Do you remember our server's name?"

"Mary. It was Mary."

"And the cookies spell?"

"Me. They spell Me. Wood U Mary Me. Would you marry me? Is that what you're trying to say?" Jackson got down on his knees and pulled out the ring.

"Theresa Rizzo, I love you so much and want to spend my life with you. Would you marry me?"

Theresa jumped out of her seat and let out a shriek. "Yes. Yes, of course, I'll marry you! Oh Jacky, I love you so much! This is the best night ever." Jackson slipped the ring onto her finger. It was a perfect fit. Customers at nearby tables applauded and Mary came out with a bottle of champagne. Jackson felt like the luckiest man in the world.

Chapter 50

Susan was finishing her second cup of coffee when her phone rang. She was still trying to decide if what Amber's mother had said at the gravestone counted as a confession when her phone rang.

"Mom, it's me."

"Hi, Lynette. Is everything okay?" Susan knew her daughter's due date was quickly approaching and every time the phone rang, that's where Susan's mind went.

"I'm fine. I wanted to call with some great news. Jackson proposed to Theresa last night."

"Oh, that is wonderful news. They make a great couple. I'm so happy for them."

"Me too. Hey, I also wanted to tell you that Jackson spoke to the valet and got a written statement that Phillip was there that night and that he'd left shortly after the ceremony began."

"I'm still waiting on the lab for the DNA analysis from the cigarette butts you found outside. Are you and Dad going to the bench dedication at the school this evening?"

"We'll be there. I think it was a wonderful idea that the school had a bench made and inscribed with Amber's name."

"Let me get to work. We'll talk later."

Susan hung up with Lynette and called both Jackson and Theresa to congratulate them. Then she thought about stopping by to see Dalia. Zach's body should probably be released soon. She got dressed and headed to the Rocking Horse. When she got there, Dalia was in her room packing. She was still in her bathrobe.

"So, it looks like you'll finally be heading home," said Susan.

"Yes, the police said they'll be releasing the body soon. I'll go back to New Jersey and will work with Zach's mother and sister to plan a funeral."

"Have you decided what you're going to do now that Zach is gone? Will you stay in New Jersey?"

"I'll stay at least until the baby is born. After that, I'm not sure." Dalia's phone rang. "Excuse me a minute. I'll take this in the bathroom."

Susan looked around the room. The lid on Dalia's suitcase was shut, but not zipped. Susan couldn't resist taking a peek. She let out a gasp when she saw what was inside.

Chapter 51

It was definitely feeling like November. Susan pulled her coat tighter. Mike put his arm around her. Judging by the crowd gathered around at the bench dedication, no one would have guessed how unpopular Amber had been. Students, faculty, friends, and family members came out in droves to honor Amber Bernstein. The school principal gave a short speech, followed by the Bernsteins thanking the school for their thoughtfulness. Several friends shared memories and many tears were shed. Jackson and Theresa were there. Susan was surprised, but pleased that Dalia and Phillip had come. Dalia had told her she wanted to pay her respects but Susan had doubted that she'd show up.

"Julie, Joey, how are things going? Enjoying your freedom, Tank?" asked Susan. Tank had his arm around Julie. Julie had gone back to her natural light hair color and Susan thought that she was looking especially pretty these days.

"I feel like a truck has been lifted off my chest. I can't even tell you how much I'm appreciating my freedom," said Tank. Susan saw him squeeze Julie's waist.

"I see your hand is no longer bandaged Joey," said Susan.

"Yep. It's good as new. Just in time for volleyball season." Most of the crowd had already dispersed when Jackson called a small group together in front of the school.

"Julie, Joey, Mr. and Mrs. Bernstein, come over here for a few minutes. "Dalia, Phillip, don't go just yet."

"What's this about?" asked Dalia. She looked around. She was twisting the fringes of her scarf around her fingers.

"I have some important news to share," said Jackson. He stood up tall and cleared his throat. "We have identified Zach's killer."

There were audible gasps and stunned expressions. Jackson paused long enough to create additional suspense, then continued. He turned to Julie.

"Julie Martin; I mean Kaitlyn Chichester, you had a strong motive for killing Zach, but an eyewitness has placed you inside the house while Zach was still alive on the patio. Luckily for you, the Martin family is not going to press charges against you for stealing their daughter's identity."

"Thank God," said Julie/Kaitlyn. "I did steal Julie's identity, but of course, I didn't kill Zach. I'm glad you know that now. And I'll be sure to thank Julie's parents." Jackson moved on.

"Dalia Chichester, you had similar reasons for wanting Zach dead but you also have been cleared by an eye witness," said Jackson. He glanced at Theresa, thankful that she'd been able to help him with the case by placing Dalia inside the house while Zach was still alive on the patio.

"If I had wanted Zach dead, I'd have killed him long ago," said Dalia. "Besides, I could never murder the father of my baby." She stopped twisting her scarf fringe and patted her barely visible baby bump. Phillip glared at her, clenching his fists. Next, Jackson turned to Joey.

"Joey Martin. You received shocking news the night of the shower. News that put your mother in danger. Your temper caused you to punch the side of the Wiles' house and badly injure your hand the night of the murder. This happened while you and your girlfriend were still hiding behind the tool shed."

"How did you..."

"Carolina Rogers told us. Don't worry. It turned out to be a good thing. With the severity of your injury, it would have been nearly impossible for you to push your father into the Jacuzzi and then throw in the boom box."

"Mr. Bernstein." The crowd now turned to stare at him. "You probably had the strongest motive of all for murder. Zachary Chichester killed your only child. You admitted to being at the shower the night of the murder. Several witnesses saw someone lurking behind the patio. There were reports of a man's voice being heard out on the patio. Cigarette butts were found outside the Wiles' house and you're a smoker." Gasps came from the crowd. Jackson stood tall with his chest puffed out like a penguin. All eyes were on him as he continued.

"Fortunately for you, the DNA on the cigarette butts was not yours. It matched someone else. Someone who stood to gain financially. Someone who needed Zach out of the way so he could be with the supposed mother of his child. Someone whose alibi was proven to be false."

"You mean it wasn't you?" Mrs. Bernstein turned to her husband incredulously. "I thought you did it, Robert. After I made you go over to that woman's house and..."

"No, it wasn't me, Rebecca," he said, "but I wish it had been. I envy the person who crushed the life out of that monster." He put his arms around his wife and placed his chin against the top of her head.

"So do I," whispered Rebecca Bernstein between sobs.

"Who was it?" asked Bernstein, looking over at Jackson. The crowd looked around at each other. There was a silence. Jackson spoke slowly and deliberately. "It was Zach's business partner. It was Phillip Bachman." With a dramatic flair, Jackson pointed at Phillip.

Someone gasped. Amongst the crowd, eyes opened wide and mouths gaped.

"We determined that you had indeed been at the Chamber of Commerce awards ceremony the night of the murder, but we have a witness who gave a sworn deposition stating that he brought your car to you shortly after the ceremony began. Should I go on? Here's another thing. My partner discovered that you have been embezzling money from the company for years and sending it to an off-shore account." There were more gasps from the crowd. Jackson was obviously enjoying the attention, taking his time revealing each new piece of evidence.

"And the most incriminating evidence of all—the DNA found on the cigarette butts matched yours." Jackson pointed his index finger at Phillip.

"That still isn't proof that I committed the murder." Suddenly, Phillip bolted through the crowd, trying to escape.

"Stop in the name of the law," cried Jackson. Susan imagined Jackson practicing that line over and over again in his bathroom mirror. Susan had often thought that if Jackson hadn't become a detective, he would have had a good shot at being an actor.

Tank, who'd been standing next to Julie the whole time, took off after Phillip. It wasn't long before Tank caught up to him and tackled him to the ground. Jackson caught up several minutes later and snapped the cuffs on Phillip.

"Nice work," said Jackson.

"I haven't run like that since my days as a linebacker for the Westbrook High Cougars," replied Tank.

Phillip wasn't making Jackson's job easy. He wriggled and pulled, trying to get out of the cuffs. He was shouting, "I'm not going down alone for this." He pointed at Dalia. "She was the mastermind. She planned the whole thing. She made me do it."

"Shut your trap. You're making things worse for yourself. If I were you, I wouldn't say a word without your lawyer present," said Jackson. He started leading him toward the cruiser.

"Wait," shouted Susan, stepping to the front of the group. Now all eyes were focused on her. "He's right. There's more to this story. Dalia did put him up to it."

"That's ridiculous," said Dalia. "Why would I do such a thing?" Once again, she twisted the scarf fringe around her fingers.

Susan turned to her. "You were romantically involved with Phillip, or at least you were pretending to be. When you came to the shower, you said you were almost late because you had a last minute phone call. I was pretty sure that call was to Phillip. My guess is that you told him something to inflame the situation. Did you tell him Zach had found out about your affair, or maybe that Zach threatened you?"

"That's total fiction. I did no such thing," insisted Dalia.

"There's no use denying it. My daughter looked up your phone records and we have confirmation that you called him. She also found that you were a co-signer on those off-shore accounts."

"That still proves nothing."

"Perhaps you called Phillip and told him Zach was going to reveal the truth about Julie that night. You told him not to let it happen because it would blow your plan to pieces. If Julie and Joey knew the truth, perhaps they'd try to claim the insurance money. Since Julie was still alive, perhaps your marriage to Zach would have been invalid, leaving you without a cent from him or the big house in Saddle River."

"I still would have had the money from the offshore accounts."

"Not if Phillip found out the truth."

"What truth?" said Dalia.

"That you had planned to get him to do the dirty work all along. You had no intention of staying with Phillip once Zach was dead. You wanted him to get arrested."

"That's absurd. I love Phillip. I would not have chosen to raise our baby all alone," said Dalia.

"That brings me to one last thing." The entire group was staring at Susan. "You aren't even pregnant. When you took that phone call in your hotel room that day, I peeked inside your suitcase and guess what I saw?"

"Tell me," said Dalia.

"Birth control pills. You were faking the whole pregnancy, allowing both Phillip and Zach to think they were the father. You were playing both of them. And another thing. I found a one-way ticket to Rio de Janeiro. A single ticket." She wagged her index finger at Dalia. "You had no intention of taking Phillip along with you."

"You bitch!" yelled Phillip.

Jackson stepped forward. He put a pair of cuffs on Dalia and led the two of them to the police cruiser.

Chapter 52

"Can you believe all that went down last night?" said Mike. He and Susan were enjoying a leisurely breakfast.

"That Dalia was quite the conniver. What a piece of work. I'm so glad that Julie, I mean *Kaitlyn*, and Joey are free from worry. I think things are heating up between Kaitlyn and Tank."

"It's about time Tank found some happiness," said Mike. "I have to admit I'm proud of you for putting together Dalia's plan. Are you going over to Lynette's today?"

"Yes. I'm going to help her organize the baby clothes in the new dresser. Jason put together the changing table last week. The room is just about ready for our grandbaby." Susan rubbed her hands together.

"Well, have fun. I'll see you at dinner." Mike kissed Susan and went to work. Susan cleared the breakfast dishes and headed to Lynette's.

"You doing okay?" asked Susan when she arrived. Her daughter had dark circles under her eyes and was rubbing her lower back.

"I sure am. Can't wait to pop this little one out though. Great job on the case, Mom. I doubt we would have ever found out that Dalia was faking the pregnancy. I'm sure she thought Phillip would go to jail and she'd be scot-free––rich and living in Rio de Janiero."

"Well, justice was done. Now, maybe Julie, I mean *Kaitlyn*, and Tank can be happy. Maybe they'll even get married one day. Speaking of which, have Jackson and Theresa set a date?"

"Not yet. They're thinking summer though. Theresa is free then and things tend to slow down at the station during the summer months."

"That's wonderful. Let's get to work on those baby clothes," said Susan.

"Mom. We'd better hurry. I think my water just broke."

Chapter 53

"Oh, my gosh. Where's your bag? Call Jason. Did you pack diapers?" Susan was speaking quickly and pacing around the room in circles.

"Calm down, Mom. The contractions haven't even.....*ouch*...I take that back. I'm pretty sure that was a contraction."

"Let's go then," said Susan. She looked around for Lynette's bag. She was so excited that she dropped the car keys. She called Jason and Mike from the car and sped to the hospital. They whisked Lynette away to labor and delivery while Susan waited for the guys.

"Where is she?" Jason came running through the hospital doors. His hair was damp with sweat. "Is she okay?"

"They took her back. Tell the nurse at the counter and they'll bring you to her. Good luck. Come out and tell us the minute that baby is here," said Susan. The door had barely swung closed when Mike came in.

"Susan, where is she?" asked Mike. He was breathing hard. Susan could tell that he'd run all the way from the parking lot.

"She's in the back with Jason. All we can do now is wait. I can't stand it."

"Do you want some coffee or anything?"

"I think the last thing I need right now is caffeine." They waited for hours. Susan tried to distract herself, taking out her phone and opening her kindle app. She couldn't focus on the story and kept rereading the same page. Mike tried to play a game on his phone. Susan kept hearing the sound that indicated he'd lost a round.

Obviously his mind was also elsewhere too. After a while, Jason came out. They ran over to him.

"She's six centimeters dilated and the contractions are coming every few minutes. It won't be too much longer," said Jason. He went back to Lynette. More hours passed. Mike was pacing; Susan drank luke warm coffee. Jason came out a second time. Susan's heart pounded. Was her grandbaby here now?

"She's nine centimeters. She'll be pushing soon." Jason looked sweaty and tired.

"I can't stand the waiting," said Susan. She picked at her cuticles.

"We don't have much choice," said Mike. "Did you call Evan and tell him?"

"Yes, I did. He's really excited and wants to be here so bad. Sometimes St. Louis just seems so far away."

"He's coming home for Thanksgiving next week. He'll meet his new niece or nephew soon enough. I can't stand this waiting. Did you make a decision about finding your birth mom?" Susan knew this was his attempt to distract her from the anticipation.

"I think I'm going to do it. Once Lynette recovers and things settle down a little, she'll know the best way to go about it." Jason came bursting through the door into the waiting room. He was smiling from ear to ear." Susan and Mike immediately accosted him.

"Well?" said Susan.

"Is Lynette okay? Is the baby okay?"

"They are both doing great. What a miracle I just witnessed!" Jason was grinning from ear to ear.

"Well, is it a boy or a girl?" said Susan. Jason took a deep breath.

"It's a healthy eight pound……..

THE END

ABOUT THE AUTHOR

 Diane Weiner is a mother of four and a veteran public school teacher with a broad range of teaching experience. She has previously published several music education articles as well as a doctoral dissertation but finds writing fiction to be much more fun. Her first cozy mystery was *Murder Is Elementary*. Westbrook, NY, the fictional setting of her Susan Wiles Schoolhouse mysteries, bears remarkable similarities to the small town in upstate New York where Diane grew up. She currently resides in South Florida with her husband of many years, their youngest daughter, two cats, and a bisch-a-poo. When not writing, Diane enjoys long distance running and spending time with her family.